ONLY TRUE IN FAIRY TALES

Eloise Blake has been fascinated by Prospect House, the shadowy romantic Gothic edifice opposite hers, ever since she moved to the village of Hookfield. When its new owner turns out to be bestselling crime author Ross Farrell, whose work is grounded in gritty reality rather than happy endings, she is determined to concentrate on her tapestry design business and her rescue dog Gracie. Love, she thinks, is only true in fairy tales. But is Ross the Prince Charming she thought didn't exist — or is he a beast in disguise?

CHRISTINE STOVELL

ONLY
TRUE IN
FAIRY TALES

LINFORD
Leicester

First published in Great Britain in 2014 by
Choc Lit Limited
Surrey

First Linford Edition
published 2018
by arrangement with
Choc Lit Limited
Surrey

A catalogue record for this book is available
from the British Library.

ISBN 978–1–4448–3782–7

Published by
F. A. Thorpe (Publishing)
Anstey, Leicestershire

Set by Words & Graphics Ltd.
Anstey, Leicestershire
Printed and bound in Great Britain by
T. J. International Ltd., Padstow, Cornwall

This book is printed on acid-free paper

To my sister, Tracy, with love.

Acknowledgements

Heartfelt thanks to the Choc Lit Team and my fellow ChocLiteers and, as always to my family, especially Tom, Caroline and Jennifer.

We had a few dogs when I was growing up, but the one I loved the most was a miniature dachshund named Zorba, who caused my sister great distress when he gobbled up every inhabitant of her doll's house in a single sitting. He was a great hunter and destroyer of footwear and was the only living creature to stick his nose in my dad's empty slippers and survive. Zorba's spirit lives on in this book.

Gracie the greyhound has lived in my imagination for many years so it was lovely to tell her story at last. For further reading about living with rehomed greyhounds, I'd recommend *Hounds at Home* by Victoria Kingston & Hilary Johnson.

1

The frosty path twinkled under a sprinkling of fairy lights as Eloise Blake followed it from the gate to beneath the Moorish fretwork porch. At the front door she hesitated. She could still turn her back on the music and laughter radiating from within if she liked, but as soon as her hand touched the bell, there'd be no choice but to cross the threshold into an unfamiliar world, where she'd be forced to exchange her coat for a glass of wine, a handful of peanuts and the company of strangers. Was it worth it just to satisfy her curiosity?

'Come on, girl, watcha waiting for? Hurry up and get in.'

Eloise was almost glad to have some company, for once, even if it was only Nigel who worked — or, more accurately, passed the time chewing gum

1

and flicking through the lads' mags — at the petrol station. But she was less delighted when he clamped his arm round her waist as the front door opened and pushed her inside first. She took off her coat and Nigel pinched her bottom.

'Looking good tonight, girl. On your own again then?'

Eloise glared at him.

'You want to loosen up a bit,' he sulked. 'It's a party not a bloody wake.'

Eloise winced and was about to put her coat back on when the crowds parted to reveal a leggy blonde in a perfect little black dress and strappy high-heels holding court. Nigel raised his hand and waggled his fingers at her in a fawning wave. Dragging Eloise with him, he bore down on her purposefully. The blonde looked faintly appalled before recognition dawned.

'Oh!' she said, 'the guy from the garage. Neil, isn't it?'

Nigel was too busy puckering up to correct her. He lunged at the blonde who sidestepped him neatly. 'And you've brought your partner. How lovely! I'm Kym,' she announced holding out a tiny, beautifully manicured hand.

'Actually, Nigel and I are nothing to do with each other,' Eloise quickly explained, trying not to cringe. 'We just happened to arrive at the same time. I'm Eloise Blake. I live at the end of the terrace opposite — Blenheim Cottages?'

'I *love* those little Victorian houses,' Kym trilled. 'They're just adorable aren't they?'

But not so adorable that she actually wanted to buy one, Eloise noted.

'Ross will be so pleased to meet you. He's been so busy I doubt if he'd even have recognised his previous neighbours,' Kym went on, 'it'll do him good to live somewhere where the pace is slower.'

Eloise thought fleetingly of the line of cars trying to turn on to the main road for Ebbesham every morning and

3

wondered if the women on school, station or supermarket runs would agree.

'He's really looking forward to becoming part of the community; running a stall at the church fete or taking part in the annual pantomime or whatever,' she beamed.

No, thought Eloise, she wasn't joking. She really meant it. Fifty-five minutes down the A3 and she thought she was in Merrie England, no doubt anticipating young girls dancing round the maypole or little boys kicking inflated pigs' bladders along the street.

Ever since the 'sold' board had gone up, speculation in the village about who had been brave or foolish enough to take on Prospect House was rife. In the local convenience store, whilst Eloise had been sending a parcel via Mrs Khan at the post office counter, she hadn't been in the slightest bit surprised to hear Nigel spreading the latest gossip to Mr Khan, who was packing groceries.

'He paid cash for that place, you know. Must be nice having that kind of money sloshing about. You should 'ave seen the bird he had in the car with him an' all. Some blokes get all the luck,' Nigel had reported, his face falling for a moment before he leaned closer adding, 'tell you what though, mate, she's got a nice set of headlights. 'Ave a lookout for her, mate! It'll make a change to 'ave a decent bit of crumpet round the village.'

Mrs Khan's serene face had flickered slightly as she gave Eloise her change but despite their communal thought, Nigel had still managed to saunter out of the shop without dropping dead.

'Of course, the house was in a dreadful state of neglect,' said Kym, jerking her out of her reverie. 'There were days when I despaired of ever realising my vision for it, but I think it came together perfectly in the end, don't you?'

Looking around at the carefully placed furniture and the blonde-on-blonde colour scheme, Eloise thought wistfully of scatter cushions and piles of books, and deep sofas on old Persian rugs. Struggling to find something appreciative to say, she finally remarked on how spacious the room looked.

'Simplicity is the key,' Kym pronounced. 'The right objects in the right place and so forth. Personally, I still believe that good feng shui creates good fortune and poor feng shui can make a home feel very uncomfortable.'

Her designer chairs must have the same effect, thought Eloise, since no one seemed to be sitting in them. Kym must have seen her glazing over and suddenly remembered her duties as a hostess.

'Champagne's just coming round,' she said, with a confidence Eloise didn't share as she caught sight of the waiter lurching through the other guests and recognised one of Hookfield's pierced and tattooed teenaged layabouts, press-ganged into a stiff white shirt and seemingly hell-bent on keeping the tray to himself. 'Or there are other drinks in the kitchen. I think Ross's out there at the moment,' she told Nigel. 'Would you mind doing the honours?'

Nigel, sidling further into Kym's body space, appeared rooted and only dragged his eyes off her long enough to mutter, 'Fetch us a tin of lager whilst you're there, would you, darlin'?' to Eloise.

A quick glance at the throng in the stainless steel nightmare that was the kitchen and Eloise decided she could probably skip the drink. And if Ross was anything like Kym she wasn't in a hurry to meet him either. This was exactly why she never went to parties. It was all that trying to avoid being held captive by people you hardly knew and cared about even less.

But that wasn't why she'd accepted the invitation. Prospect House, an Edwardian folly dominated by a romantic Gothic turret, was quite unlike any of its neighbours. It was secluded yet, as the sales particulars boasted, commanded magnificent views of the surrounding Downs. Fringed on one side by gnarled trees and wayward brambles, it had remained uninhabited since the death of the former elderly occupant and looked, in some lights, as if it would only require some intrepid prince to come crashing through the undergrowth in search of a sleeping beauty to turn it into an enchanted castle. In other lights it seemed bleaker, more Gormenghast than Brothers Grimm. Or perhaps she was just a tad cynical, these days, about the type of man who turned up at your door unannounced to tell you that he'd come to change your world.

Yet the mysterious house opposite had certainly cast its spell over her. When she'd moved into her own modest home opposite two years earlier, there were dark days when it still seemed as if she was living her life on autopilot, but even then her interest had been piqued by shadowy, romantic Prospect House. Cheryl had been right to accuse her of being unable to resist the opportunity of a legitimate snoop. 'You've been dying to get round there ever since the 'sold' board went up,' her sister had teased, 'fretting about what all those men spilling out of white vans were doing to the place. I don't know why you didn't put in a silly offer for it yourself.'

'I think the idea is for the executors to accept the best offer, not the silliest,' Eloise had pointed out, thinking of the bank's rather large stake in her own property.

Disappointingly, everything she'd seen so far was much too clinical for her taste, but what she'd always wanted to do was to climb the tower and see what the view across the Downs was like from up there. And when else would she get the chance? Glancing round first to make sure no one was watching, she made a hasty beeline across the hall.

★　★　★

After all the anticipation, Eloise was disappointed to find that the turret bedroom at the top was just as puritanical in style as the floor below. Seemingly devoid of personal objects, the room was dominated by a modern cast-iron, four-poster bed, draped with muslin. What could have been a unique and intimate space was as artfully contrived as an advertisement for the latest designer fragrance. All it required was a tasteful arrangement of bodies and limbs on white linen, dappled with coloured light from the stained glass windows to complete the tableau. What place was there, Eloise wondered, for semen, blood or tears in this cold and sterile chamber?

She would have chosen something far less restrained like dazzling walls of lapis lazuli blue perhaps, for a sensuous and seductive feel by night. Or maybe a rosy pink, like the colour of dawn? Her gaze rested on a pair of glazed doors that opened to the narrow cast-iron balcony girdling the tower — she imagined waking up to watery sun shimmering through them and conjured up comparisons with the faded grandeur of a crumbling Venetian palazzo. Something romantic, something wild, somewhere to sleep, to dream, to make love — how did that creep in? Eloise shook her head. Romance was for starry-eyed girls, something she'd grown out of, along with the tooth fairy and Father Christmas, and her blissful bed was the place where she got a good night's sleep.

But having come this far, it would be a pity not to go all the way and do what she'd been so longing to do since she'd first set eyes on Prospect House. The key in the double doors to the balcony turned easily, and with a gentle push on the handle, she was free to step outside. Half-light and the cold air rushing to greet her intensified the raw sensation of height and, for a moment, she was frozen to the wall. Uppermost in her mind, as she detached herself somewhat warily from the brickwork, was the thought that given Prospect House's years of neglect, she probably shouldn't rely too much on the iron balustrade for support.

But what a viewpoint! Below her the garden was full of shadows. Scraps of conversation fluttered up from the party and were lost on the wind. And as her eyes adjusted, bright stars began to emerge in the sapphire sky, dancing above the melancholy shadows of the Downs, dazzling in their intensity and so close that she almost felt she could touch them.

Something of an expert on experiences described as 'character forming', Eloise had learned to keep a close guard on her emotions, but even she was alive to the spellbinding beauty of the night. Others, less cynical than her, might have allowed it to stir their imaginations and suppose it to be full of possibilities. What could happen, they might have said, on a night like this? But before Eloise could suspend her disbelief, a hideous creak beneath her hands broke the magic and alerted her to the fact that she was unwisely craning over the rail. She pulled back hastily before she pushed her luck, or the balcony, any further.

Her illicit wander round Prospect House had, if nothing else, provoked no stirrings of envy and shown her that she really was quite settled. Being alone wasn't nearly as lonely as the deep divide of a shared bed when you were staring at the wall of someone's back. It wasn't *being* wanted that counted, it was knowing what *you* wanted. Recognising your own needs. She didn't need a crumbling castle and she didn't need a handsome prince. What she wanted was what she'd got: a balanced life, an enjoyable routine and no complications. Threading her way round to the sanctuary of the tower, she reached the door with some relief, closed it behind her, and stepped into the barrier of a solid male chest.

'Jesus!' gulped Eloise, as the light went on, temporarily blinding her.

'I'm flattered, but Ross will do,' a low voice murmured amiably.

Eloise found herself gazing up into a strong, lived-in face and smoky grey eyes.

'Hello,' he said, watching her with amused interest. 'I'm Ross Farrell. Aren't you enjoying my party?'

'Eloise,' she mumbled, trying to ignore the part of her brain that had just started sending frantic signals ordering her libido to come out of hibernation. 'Eloise Blake. It's nothing personal but I only really came to see what you'd done to Prospect House.'

'You and half of Hookfield,' he agreed. 'Fortunately Kym's as eager to show the place off as everyone else is to see it. For my part I've had enough conversations on the subject of interior design to last a lifetime and I'm certainly past caring about the relative merits of 'echo chic', 'retro' or 'bright 'n' funky,'' he grumbled, shaking his head at the stark four-poster and the practically bare room. 'You've no idea how difficult it's been hanging on to the old Chesterfield in my study,' he confided. 'Kym's always got her eye on it. That sofa's been with me since my first flat. God knows what she finds so objectionable about it.'

As Ross fell into a thoughtful silence, Eloise was about to make her excuses and creep away when he seemed to remember she was there. 'Well, now that you've finished the tour,' he said with a grin, 'let me get you a drink.'

Letting him lead her down the stairs, Eloise had time to reflect on her narrow escape. Ross was clearly far too busy with other matters to react in, what most people would deem, the appropriate manner at finding a total stranger gallivanting round their bedroom. He was also, she noted gratefully, too preoccupied to notice her blushing like a schoolgirl. Yes, Ross Farrell was just the sort of man fate would send along as a sharp reminder not to tempt it. So you think you can control your emotions, stem the tide of cravings and desires, it seemed to be saying. Well, try this for size.

And the worst thing about it, she thought, with an appreciative glance at her host's tall frame — the lean hips lovingly moulded by vintage jeans, and his broad shoulders flexing beneath a loose-fitting white shirt — was that she found the idea shockingly appealing. Except that she hadn't clawed her way to some semblance of normality to risk a messy entanglement right on her doorstep. Especially not now, when she was feeling settled at last. So, even if the fragrant and talented Kym upset him one more time by removing every stick of furniture in the house in the name of fashion, and Ross Farrell crawled across the road on his hands and knees and begged her to let him in, she'd steer clear, wouldn't she?

Feeling thoroughly pulled together, she prepared to return to the now throbbing body of the party when Ross took an unexpected turn and opened another door. 'Come on in,' he invited.

2

One look at the battered brown leather Chesterfield and Eloise knew exactly why Kym objected to it. In contrast to the austere desk and a very professional working area on one side of the room, the sofa looked distinctly louche and a little too redolent of rampant shag-fests *du temps perdu*.

'Make yourself comfortable,' Ross invited.

Eloise gave only a fleeting thought to how many women had done just that on this spot in the past and tried to fold herself into as small a space as possible, feeling like the village idiot Ross probably thought she was. It was bad enough being caught wandering round his bedroom but how, she thought as he switched on a couple of low lamps, could she not have recognised him?

No one with even a flicker of interest

in popular fiction could fail to miss those compelling features staring moodily out from one of the prominent displays in bookshops everywhere. A direct gaze that dared you to come closer at your peril, soft Byronic curls that made you want to try — regardless of the consequences. Eloise had put seductive publicity shots down to cunning lighting and a sympathetic photographer, but she had to admit, with a sinking feeling, that the enigma in the flesh wasn't so bad either.

Usually described as 'darkly humorous', his clutch of clever, stylish thrillers had spawned a series of gritty TV spinoffs. Eloise had sat through an episode one evening, but had felt the need to cheer herself up with some Jilly Cooper before she could turn out the light. However beautifully crafted and blackly funny other people found Ross Farrell's work, it was much too disturbing for her taste.

Swiftly scanning his bookshelves, she looked for textbooks on forensic medicine, criminal trials or any evidence to show that the stuff didn't just come out of his head. After all, what kind of personality would invent such gruesome scenarios, she asked herself, with another quick glance at her host. Noting the amusement flickering in his eyes and in the small smile that lifted the corners of his mouth, softening his brooding expression, she began to wonder exactly why he had brought her to his study.

'So, Eloise Blake,' he said, his deep voice gruff as he handed her a drink. 'Are you a professional nosy parker or do you do anything else with your time?'

Despite the blunt question, his eyes were surprisingly warm and friendly. Deciding it was probably safe to assume she wasn't there to play out a scene in his next book, Eloise knocked back a couple of fingers of Scotch and, feeling somewhat revived, concluded that a straight answer would be the best defence. 'I design tapestries.'

'Really?' Ross's dark eyebrows shot up and the corners of his mouth twitched. 'How quaint.'

'Yes, well, you probably would say that.'

'Oh?'

'Well, your line of work is stabbed bodies rather than stabbing canvas. I expect it does sound rather twee to you.'

His stern features were lifted by a sudden grin, 'I might press flowers in my spare time for all you know.'

Eloise shot him a look that showed she rather doubted it.

Laughing, he shook his head. 'You'd believe it if I wrote romantic novels, I bet. Sure, I write about the dark side of human nature but that doesn't make me a nasty person,' he went on. 'I work in a competitive industry. I have to create an original product and I have to market it. If you really believed that I was as evil as one of my characters you wouldn't be sitting here with me now, would you?'

Leaning back against the leather sofa, he held her gaze until Eloise was annoyed to feel herself blushing.

'It's only fiction,' he went on softly. 'Fairy tales for grown-ups, like Beauty and the Beast or Little Red Riding Hood. What big teeth you have, Grandmother, and all that.'

Trying not to think too much about being gobbled up, Eloise attempted to steer the conversation in a more serious direction. 'Don't you ever worry about the consequences of what you write?'

'You think my readers will all go out and copy what's in my books?' he scoffed. 'Believe me, those sorts of people don't need to read books for their inspiration. They do what they do anyway. Oh, they might try to justify their actions by citing this influence or that, but it doesn't have to be something they've read, it could be something they've seen or something they've simply taken a dislike to.' He gave her a bad boy grin. 'I daresay some of them even dream up their ideas when they're stabbing away at their tapestries.'

'Designer tapestries may not have the

same cachet as designer violence but at least I'm trying to create something beautiful,' Eloise sniffed.

'Come on, Eloise,' he teased. 'You can't jump to conclusions about me and not expect me to fight back a little? I mean, I associate tapestries with charming chintzy scenes and maiden aunts, but does that make you prim and proper?'

Something went awry with the extinguishing glare she'd intended for him when she looked up and met the provocative challenge in his storm-grey eyes. She wanted to laugh, but it was hard enough to breathe when he was looking at her like that, daring her to buck the stereotype. Just because he was so full of himself, every bit the successful author, with his arms stretched along the back of the sofa and his head tilted back so that his dark hair touched the collar of his white shirt, why should she care? What did it matter to her if he thought she was demure and old-fashioned?

Living quietly, untroubled by rampant hormones and heartbreak, was far more peaceful than sitting here now feeling the heat rise in her body simply because a man was staring at her with an intensity that made her feel as if she was the last woman on the planet. And she could certainly do without some long-lost nerve endings picking this moment to emerge from dormancy, tingling as if yearning to spring into action.

Some annoying reflex action made her drop her gaze to his mouth and a little voice observed that it was a shame it was so far away from her. A mouth like that, she reckoned, ought not to keep itself to itself. But that would be madness, wouldn't it? Reckless. She couldn't remember the last time she'd kissed a stranger at a party and yet . . . He shifted and his arm dropped lower, almost touching her. He moved a little closer, all body heat and danger, and she thought she heard, from somewhere in the distance, the crash of breaking glass. It was either that or the sound of her guard dropping, but whatever it was, her common sense heard it too. Taking a deep breath as she eventually found the right words, she was about to speak when the door flew open and someone said her lines for her.

'Ross! What the heck do you think you're playing at?'

As Kym's head swivelled in her direction, Eloise found herself being regarded with a stare as chilly as a dip in dry-ice. When followed up with a haughty head-to-toe appraisal, Eloise was afraid that, given a light tap, she'd probably shatter into a million pieces. Gratefully she noted that once no obvious competition had been detected, Kym's expression defrosted a little.

'I should have known Ross had found a willing victim to bore about his books,' she said, ruffling his curls. Her own beautifully cut hair swung exactly into place as she straightened up and turned to Eloise. 'He'll monopolise anyone patient enough to give him the slightest encouragement so it's sweet of you to listen when you could be having a good time. I expect poor Nigel will be wondering where you are, too.'

She turned back to Ross. 'Come on,' she ordered. 'I know that all these calming colours and natural fabrics were supposed to help your creative flow, but this isn't really the time to be holed up in your study, not when you've got other people waiting to meet you.'

Eloise remembered to stop opening and closing her mouth before Kym was inspired by her feng shui principles to throw her in a goldfish bowl and find a wealth corner for her to enhance. For a moment she'd been convinced that Ross was going to demonstrate some of the bad behaviour her fevered imagination believed he was capable of. Perhaps she really had designed one tapestry too many? Realising that Kym expected someone to do something, she pulled herself together and spoke.

'I really ought to get back home,' she announced, standing up. 'Thank you for a lovely evening.'

'But you've only just got here,' Kym said, raising her eyebrows.

'I know,' Eloise agreed, 'but I promised Gracie I wouldn't be long. She's only three and she doesn't really like being left alone.'

The brief, but very chilly, silence that followed was broken abruptly by the Hookfield youth, who had made such an inept waiter, dragging a giggly girl, exploding out of a tiny top, into the study.

'Oops! Sorry mate,' he said, with a nod at Ross before turning to the girl, 'there's some kind of threesome going on in this one. We'll have to find somewhere else.'

Kym yelped and shot after them with Eloise at her heels, thanking her lucky stars for the diversion. She staggered unnoticed past a heaving mass of Hookfield residents, who had now overcome their initial awe and inhibitions and were waving glasses in noisy groups, crunching on canapés and sending splatters of chilli dipping sauce flying over the pristine coir flooring.

'Bloody disgusting!' she heard someone mutter, and turned to see her least favourite neighbour, Brett Dorling-Jones, shovelling up pizza and glaring at a couple dirty-dancing in the middle of the room. 'Why is it always the ugly buggers who have to maul each other in public?' he asked his wife through a mouthful of half-chewed food, 'It turns my stomach, princess, it really does.'

Eloise took a glance at his puce face and decided to escape before the evening deteriorated any further. Ross and Kym were more of the sort of incomers the village didn't need. Even worse, they were practically guaranteed to bring a steady import of friends, filling the drive opposite with four by fours or yomping off across the Downs in brand new Barbours in the firm belief that they were reinvigorating the rural economy.

Hookfield residents, on the whole, were a quiet lot used to their village playing the poor relation to Ebbesham, a prosperous commuter town. Eloise liked the fact that people kept themselves to themselves and their heads bent against the biting wind that swept across the

Downs at this time of year. It was one of the reasons she'd chosen to live there. Unfortunately the relative isolation of the village was fast becoming its redeeming feature. People who previously rejected the place now regularly searched for 'for sale' boards there, drawn by the idea of being within striking distance of Ebbesham's facilities without joining the urban sprawl. Then they expected everyone else to celebrate.

Well, she'd seen enough. The lovely old house might look enchanting, at least from the outside, but in Ross Farrell, it came complete with its very own beast. The best thing she could do from now on was to stay well clear.

* * *

The next day Ross sat up in bed, wincing as his warm bare back met the cold iron bedstead, and watched the jewelled morning light from the stained-glass windows dance across the snowy wasteland that was now his bedroom.

'Simplicity,' Kym had decreed. 'A clear room for a clear focus.'

He rubbed his hand across the stubble on his jaw and decided to remain unshaven. Kym would probably disapprove of that too, but he couldn't be bothered and it wasn't as if smooth skin would help him write again. He was beginning to wonder what would. Finn, his off-beat detective hero, had made him a household name and earned him a lot of money. Others had profited along the way, thanks to the TV spin-off: the actor past his sell-by date whose career had been revived, the young actress who had proved herself to be more than just another pouting starlet and TV executives who could breathe again as their viewing stats soared. And then . . . nothing. From two books a year to nothing in two years, whilst rumours abounded about why the author who could do no wrong suddenly couldn't write.

Putting on a white towelling gown — another of Kym's touches — he wandered down to the kitchen where the homely painted wooden units had been replaced with surgical steel. Somehow it was easier to imagine kidneys being transplanted here than devilled, he couldn't help observe. But at least he'd hung on to his beloved Chesterfield. He chuckled to himself, thinking about the expression on his new and nosy neighbour's face when he'd diverted her into his study. He was used to glamorous women pressing their numbers into his hand at social functions, but finding one cheeky enough to hide in his bedroom made an interesting change.

It crossed his mind that his first thought of elderly spinsters stitching away at their canvasses seemed at odds with Eloise Blake. All those sinuous flowing lines of her berry-red dress reminded him of a medieval damsel. In another age she would have made a wonderful model for the Lady of Shalott.

'There she weaves by night and day, a magic web with colours gay,' Ross murmured to himself. This damsel in distress hadn't wasted any time in leaving her loom for the chance to look round Prospect House though — and got more than she'd bargained for, he thought, recalling her shocked gasp as she walked into him and the warmth of her soft feminine curves pressed against his chest. Those curves had looked very inviting, sitting on the sofa next to him like that, but fate — and Kym — had intervened in the nick of time.

From the consternation in her clear blue eyes when Eloise had surveyed his study, anyone would think he was as much of a beast as she seemed to imagine. Certainly all that softness and heat so close to him had brought out some of his base instincts, but evidently there was something much more solid than a mysterious curse preventing Eloise Blake from having fun. She'd left her child at home alone. As Kym remarked later, pointing to the terraced-house opposite, living two minutes away was no excuse for the woman's behaviour. What sort of cold-hearted mother did that? No wonder she'd fled the housewarming party in such a hurry; her conscience must finally have caught up with her.

Casting his troubled eye over disciplined rows of glass jars already lining up on the scrubbed shelves, he brewed coffee which he drank from a white china cup. Staring out at the twisted trunks and tangled branches of the wooded tracks of the Downs, he began to wonder if cutting himself off to live in the country would really suit him if he was already so desperate for excitement that he'd come close to making a clumsy pass at the first attractive woman to cross his path. He blew out a deep breath, thanking his lucky stars at a narrow escape when a movement in the bushes made him start . . . and suddenly his new neighbour didn't seem even faintly amusing. Not content with making herself at home in his bedroom, she was there now, cowering in the undergrowth pointing a camera at him.

3

Wearing fingerless gloves to try to keep her hands warm, Eloise fervently hoped that the surrounding foliage cloaked her from anyone who might be looking out of Prospect House. Otherwise they'd be wondering what she was doing, squatting in the bushes. She could just imagine Kym telling her smart friends, 'So after I'd prised her off Ross at the party, we then caught her the next morning hiding in the bushes waiting for her next opportunity!'

Having captured the images she needed to remind her of the details she might otherwise forget, Eloise hunkered down even lower, worried that anyone catching sight of her would think she was having a wee. The trouble was that these particular whorls of soft green foxglove foliage, pushing through brown leaves shiny with frost or pink and papery with age, were perfect for the basis of a tapestry she had in mind: 'Prelude to Spring', with all the promise of new growth but with silver threads to suggest the chilly days still lingering.

Whenever her knack of seeing a quirky twist of nature as a web of wool kicked in, Eloise felt a simultaneous sense of amazement that, after such a prolonged downward spiral, luck had finally turned in her favour. If she hadn't needed some money pretty sharpish she would never have accepted her sister's offer of work in Aquarius, her quirky craft shop. And if Cheryl hadn't persuaded her to do something with what Eloise only thought of as a hobby, her tapestry designs would have remained undiscovered by the manufacturer who commissioned her work, screen-printed it and sold it in kit form. Occasionally, when she looked at one of the glossy packages, with their stiff canvasses and numbered skeins of coloured wool, she was reminded that, in death, Seb had unwittingly set her free.

As a sudden shadow fell across her

notepad, Eloise's first thought was for Gracie. When they'd first been introduced, Gracie had been so nervous and wary of everyone, so lacking in self-esteem, that she'd hung back, barely capable of making eye contact. Eloise, still a traumatised and hanky-wringing mess herself then, wasn't at all convinced that adopting a retired greyhound was a sensible idea. Looking into Gracie's sad face though, she'd recognised a kindred wounded spirit and hadn't been able to walk away.

Now, as Eloise's apprehensive gaze travelled over long legs in scruffy jeans and upwards, across a broad chest, her mouth went dry at the sight of her new neighbour's angry expression.

'Just what the heck is your problem?' he growled, looming over her. 'Why are you spying on me?'

'I wasn't spying,' she gulped, waving a sketchpad at him like a white flag. The shame of being taken for a voyeur rendered her speechless for a long moment until she could frame the words to defend herself. When she could manage to speak, everything tumbled out in a rush. 'I *am* working, honestly. Have a look at the pictures if you want proof. The camera just helps me remember the colours, but it's the pencil drawings that enable me to form the composition. This is where I get my ideas; from what I see here on the Downs and in the natural world around me.'

'Leaving your little girl alone in the house again, I suppose?'

Eloise shook her head. What was he going on about? And why hadn't Gracie reacted?

'You have been told, haven't you,' the homing organiser at the kennels had warned her when Eloise had gone to choose a dog, 'that she can be quite anxious with men?'

'Not a problem,' Eloise replied, with all the confidence of someone who hadn't the faintest idea of what 'quite anxious' could mean. 'I'm widowed and have no plans at all to remarry.'

In return she had received a doubtful smile and a look that suggested she fully expected to see Gracie back at the kennels very soon. Of course, as Eloise quickly found out, not having a resident man was one thing, but just the sight of any male figure appearing in the same street as them was enough to send poor Gracie into an utter panic.

The first time Eloise's parents had called in to see the new arrival, Gracie had let out a blood-curdling shriek of terror at the sight of her father. The episode of shrill and incessant barking which followed, had left them all deafened and unable to think or talk and hadn't subsided until long after her parents had gone and, only then, when Gracie was completely satisfied that the dreadful monster she had spotted wasn't about to return.

Just when it seemed that it would be impossible to keep Gracie if she was ever to see her father again, Eloise's parents had turned up with Wurst, their naughty and very spoilt miniature dachshund in tow. Gracie, seemingly shamed by the sight of such a small hound so nonchalantly unaffected by the hideous bogeyman at the other end of his lead, had fallen silent, though still quivering, and had managed to cope with her fear. Happily, these days, she usually managed to control her urge to scream even when Eloise's dad turned up alone. Although there had been one or two very difficult encounters when they were out and about, Eloise was proud of how she and Gracie had muddled through the dark days together, of their mutual rescue and the slow, tentative business of repair. Now her new neighbour, standing there bristling with indignation, threatened to undo all the good work.

Panicking in case the nervous greyhound had slunk off without her noticing, or was cowering in fear in the nearest hidey-hole, she looked around hastily. To her surprise, Gracie had got to her feet and was twirling around like a supermodel in very high heels as if to show off her blue-black coat which gleamed in the watery sunshine. And then she froze.

'Oh no,' Eloise muttered, seeing Brett Dorling-Jones on the brow of the hill checking his watch, before powering towards them on the downhill stretch of his morning jog. The last time their paths had crossed on the Downs, Gracie had demonstrated her feelings about Brett in an apparent display of aggression which had shaken Eloise and left Brett making all kinds of threats about what he would do if there was a repeat performance. Eloise quickly pulled Gracie to her side, but to little avail. Whatever the reading was on Brett's heart-rate monitor, Gracie seemed intent on raising it a few beats. She let out a blood-curdling whine and lunged at him as he passed, resulting in the air turning blue with Brett's expletives.

'This is the last time I tell you,' he snarled, pumping sweat, testosterone and menace as he waggled a fat finger in Eloise's face, 'get a muzzle on that effing animal or I'll have it under the

Dangerous Dogs Act!'

'She won't hurt you,' Eloise insisted. 'Half her teeth are missing so she couldn't bite even if she wanted to. She just gets overexcited when she sees joggers. I think all those deeply tanned and muscular calves must remind her of a pair of smooth flanks moving just ahead of her from her racing days.'

'Listen,' said Brett, pushing his sweaty face closer, 'I nearly broke my effing neck last time that dog of yours got out of control.'

'Hardly!' Eloise protested. 'She made you jump and you tripped on a branch. You only had a few scrapes and bruises; you weren't seriously hurt.'

'*I* wasn't, but it won't be the same for that bastard dog if it comes near me again so don't say you haven't been warned.' Brett laughed nastily and turned to Ross, who had moved to stand guard over Gracie. 'Nice party by the way,' he added, resetting his watch.

'I'm glad you enjoyed it,' Ross said pleasantly. 'Because it'll be the last time you set foot in my house, going round making threats like that to defenceless women.'

Eloise wondered crossly which was worse: to be thought of as a crazed stalker or a helpless female?

'And what about my defenceless kids?' sneered Brett, before she could say anything about being quite capable of looking after herself, thank you. 'What about all the muck they pick up on their shoes thanks to disease-ridden shit machines like that crapping all over the place? I suppose you think you've moved here for some peace and quiet, don't you, eh? Think you're in the heart of the bleedin' country? Well, go and take a walk across the Downs right now and see how peaceful it is. Bloody weekend riders, cyclists, model aeroplanes falling out the sky and bloody irresponsible dog owners like her allowing their dogs to go round leaving something for everyone else to tread in. Try cleaning all the dog shit off three pairs of kiddies' shoes, mate, and you'd know where I'm coming from.' He paused just long enough to glare at his watch once more. 'Have a nice day.'

'Oh Gracie,' Eloise sighed, grabbing hold of her lead tightly as the dog moaned and slavered at Brett's heels as he jogged away from them, 'just leave him alone, will you?'

Gracie's molten chocolate eyes and sweet expression were as innocent as the day was long but Eloise imagined she was laughing. 'It's not funny,' she added. 'You'll get us both into trouble.'

'*Gracie?*'

Gracie wriggled her little rump in response to Ross, reminding Eloise that he was still standing there.

'Jupiter Grace was her racing name, but these days she's just plain Gracie.'

'Ah,' said Ross, 'I didn't know you were talking about a dog.'

'Who else would I mean?' Eloise asked. And then his cryptic comment fell into place. 'Surely you didn't think I'd leave a child on her own?' she demanded to know.

He rubbed his jaw sheepishly.

'You did, didn't you?'

He gave her a slow, contrite smile. You'd need a force shield to resist him if he really turned on the charm, she grudgingly admitted to herself, noticing how the light made it seem as if the dark pools of his pupils were set in circles of pewter.

'Look, I don't seem to have got off on the right foot with you somehow,' he said, as if genuinely perplexed that he didn't have her eating out of his hand. 'Why don't we start from the beginning? How about coming over for coffee?'

He was watching her; studying her with a half-smile and an air of expectation that made him stand just a little too close. All the trademarks, in fact, of a one hundred per cent guaranteed heartbreaker. The sort of man who, if she wasn't very careful, she could find completely irresistible.

With or without Kym? she almost asked, remembering another very good reason to stay away from Ross. 'Sorry,' she said instead, holding his gaze. 'Please don't think I'm being rude, I'm busy, that's all. If I don't produce any work, the bills don't get paid.'

'I don't exactly sit around watching daytime TV myself.' He smiled.

'No, I'm sure you don't,' Eloise agreed. 'How *is* the writing going?'

★　★　★

Well, his neighbour's barbed comment had certainly helped focus his attention on what he was supposed to be doing, Ross admitted, lifting his arms and stretching back in his ergonomic office chair. He was often praised for his intricately woven plots, but sitting in front of his screen, deleting one sentence after another, he found it difficult to work up any enthusiasm for his so-called 'work in progress'.

After a day of achieving nothing, he was left with a sense of emptiness that he couldn't begin to fill. He had plenty of money, an honorary degree and enough literary-ish invitations to fill his diary for a couple of years if he chose, but where was the kick in doing more of the same? If that was his future, he might just as well return to his London flat. Kym, who was currently installed there because of the demands of her own work, would simply have to get used to the idea.

He got up and prowled the house, irritated and frustrated. He was going to miss the city, not for the sake of trendy restaurants, culture and company. Once upon a time, he'd found inspiration by losing himself in the amorphous crowd or threading, unnoticed, through oily, rain-soaked streets. Where had it all gone wrong? With a sudden need for the reassurance of traffic noise and emergency sirens, he stepped out from his darkened turret room onto the balcony but only heard the distant and alienating drone of a motorway.

Looking up, he saw a sky so clear that

the constellations leapt at him from their indigo backdrop. The Hunter loomed over the house opposite, drawing Ross's gaze down to the yellow glow of what he'd worked out to be Eloise's bedroom. Instead of letting his eyes slide over the square of light to the dark arms of the Downs that embraced the village, he allowed them to linger and found himself wondering about the woman behind the veil of curtains. He remembered the dismay in her troubled blue eyes when he'd accused her of spying on him, and then — good work, Ross — of abandoning her own child in the house.

When he'd tried to make amends, Eloise reacted as if he really was some sort of psychopath and every bit as bad as some of his fictional creations. It niggled him that she'd been so quick to refuse his invitation to make up over a friendly coffee. Perhaps his swipe about tapestry designers being strait-laced had been near the mark after all; maybe Eloise would, indeed, have a fit of the vapours if touched by a man's ungloved hand? It was laughable really. Yet, somehow the laugh didn't come and Ross couldn't shrug off the image of the woman with her tousled dark hair, or the possibilities suggested by that ungloved hand.

Perhaps the tapestry imagery had started it but now he couldn't look at her without a sense of something temptingly Victorian and taboo. With her coat clutched around her, the voluminous long skirts swirling over lace-up boots, there was hardly an inch of bare flesh to be seen. Yet all those layers of clothes somehow seemed to add to her allure. He couldn't stop his mind wandering to thoughts of undressing her, like an exquisite parcel, loosening mother-of-pearl buttons, unfastening tiny hooks, slowly unbinding silk ribbon until she was white and naked before him, her dark hair rippling across his pillow.

Ross felt quite light-headed as, without warning, his entire blood supply seemed to rush to his groin. Man, his imagination needed to be set to work on a new book soon, before it started filling in any more gaps with some poor woman innocently minding her own business. Country living was going to be painful, otherwise. He was looking for stimulation, not a permanent state of arousal.

4

In Aquarius — part craft shop, part gallery, part coffee bar — on the outskirts of Ebbesham the following Monday morning, Eloise watched her sister freeze in the process of rearranging a display of delicate hand-printed silk scarves. Immediately she knew that Cheryl's sensitive radar for nosing out potential dating material had been roused by the sketchy account Eloise had given of her weekend activities.

'Ross Farrell?' Cheryl said, swivelling and gawping at her. 'Your new neighbour is Ross Farrell? No wonder you were in such a hurry to get over there. Go you!'

'He has a partner, Kym,' Eloise told her quickly, 'and you know it was the house I wanted to see, not the owner.' She could see her sister's mind working by the small furrow in her brow, which smoothed as she adjusted her expectations and cast her eye over some of the most expensive and desirable items in the shop.

'A partner who's redesigned the house from top to bottom,' she added, before Cheryl got any ideas about what she might be able to sell him. 'All those lovely period details subdued by acres of white paint and sterile steel and glass. Showy but cold and about as welcoming as a glass coffin.'

'I suppose that's appropriate, given what he writes,' Cheryl said, letting out a sigh of resignation. 'I couldn't walk under my loft hatch after watching the serial they made from his last book. I was terrified something was going to burst out and grab me. I guess you've got to be seriously warped to come up with ideas like that. Good-looking, but weird, eh? Shame.'

'Oh no, he's perfectly straightforward,' Eloise snorted as she plumped a cushion made from one of her own tapestry designs. 'Handsome, successful and thinks that now he's the lord of his own country manor, all the women in the village will be falling at his feet. This came up well, didn't it?' she gabbled, realising she'd spilled too much information.

'El-laaa?' Cheryl said, beadily, 'is there something you'd like to share with me? Please tell me he's every bit as hot as he looks. And get me an invitation to coffee soon.'

'Didn't you hear what I said?' Eloise said, shooting her a look.

'I only want him to sign a book,' Cheryl replied airily. 'You could do it for me if you like. Ask him to dedicate it to Darren, would you? I've been struggling to come up with ideas for a birthday present for him.'

'You've got to be kidding,' Eloise insisted, 'Ross Farrell's ego's already overinflated. *I'm* not going over there begging for favours.'

'Be like that then,' Cheryl grumbled, 'but I don't know why you're making such a fuss. I'm only asking you to pop in. I mean, I'll know where to find you if he's suddenly overcome with desire for you and traps you in his lair until you succumb to his lordly demands.'

Eloise inspected the cushion in close detail, but Cheryl was now too busy feeling hard done by to notice anything amiss.

'Oh very well then,' she moaned, 'in that case I'll need to make time to go shopping. You couldn't do a couple of extra days here for me, could you?'

'You're not exactly short of willing hands,' Eloise frowned, thinking of the deadline for her new collection, 'there's always one of your artists who seems to be at a loose end.'

Cheryl, slim as a reed but far less green, eyed Eloise's voluptuous figure thoughtfully. 'Hmm, I'm not sure it's the shop all those beautiful young men hanging about the place are willing to handle.'

Eloise sent the cushion flying towards her sister, but Cheryl easily ducked. It was true that Aquarius attracted a much higher percentage of talented and caring men than, say, your average exhaust fitters for example. Among the artists, jewellers and potters who turned up on a regular basis looking to showcase their work, many belonged to a particularly gorgeous species of male with soulful eyes and sensitive fingers. From Eloise's point of view it was ideal. There was no danger whatsoever of her losing her heart to any of them; they were all far nicer than the type of man she was attracted to.

'El?'

Eloise felt her mouth tighten as she recognised the tone. 'No,' she insisted, 'don't start. I'm happy as I am. Gracie's all the company I need, aren't you girl?'

The gentle greyhound, who'd been curled up at her feet, lifted her head, peering at her anxiously as she detected signs of distress.

'But it's been three years now,' Cheryl said, trying to catch her eye. 'You have to move on, El, you're throwing your life away. It might just as well have been you in that car with Seb not — '

'But it wasn't, was it?' Feeling the familiar sense of cold fingers clutching at her heart, she took a deep breath to calm herself down, for Gracie's sake.

'Look round this room,' Cheryl said, refusing to back down. 'Look at all the male artists we show in here. Look how many of them have tried to break you out of your self-imposed purdah. You might as well be stuck behind glass yourself; we can all see you, but woe betide anyone who tries to get close. Not once have you ever given any of those shy men who screw up their courage to talk to you the slightest opportunity to show you that life can be fun. I'm not asking you to marry any of them, El, but it wouldn't kill you to go on a date.'

'Depends who's driving,' Eloise said tartly, flinching as her sister gave a small cry of distress before crossing the room to hug her.

'Not all men are like Seb,' she said quietly.

Eloise held herself stiffly. She was aware of being too thin-skinned and defensive, but sometimes it was hard to know where to unbend without getting hurt. It was all right for Cheryl who'd been with Darren since forever — what did she know about heartache and pain?

'Eloise, the right man's out there. Why not give yourself a chance to believe in love again? You can't hide yourself away forever. Prince Charming's not going to come knocking on your door to find you.'

'He already did,' she replied, extricating herself gently, 'and it turns out he was great at kissing damsels in distress, but rubbish at the happy ever after. Sorry, Cheryl, but it's too late for me to start believing in fairy tales now.'

★ ★ ★

Winter seemed to have been clinging on forever this year, Eloise observed, shivering as she drove home. Or maybe it was all the constant reminders of the past preventing the permafrost around her heart from thawing. Why couldn't Cheryl leave her alone? If only her family would just accept that she was happy, she might start to believe it herself.

A fuel light glowing on the dashboard of her Focus told her it wasn't only her emotional tank that was empty. Pulling into the petrol station at the bottom of the village, having finally coaxed some life out of the car heater, Eloise was deeply reluctant to step back out into the cold. She peered hopefully through the pumps at Nigel, tucked behind the counter, but he showed no signs of being about to shift. Two years ago, when she had first moved into the area, he was forever leaning through the driver's window asking her if she would like him to fill her up. Now he was so used to her customary brush-off that he didn't even look up from ogling *Loaded* and barely managed a half-hearted 'Awright, darlin'?' as she paid.

Back in the car, she made sure that Gracie was still snug under a fleecy blanket then pulled the collar of Seb's discarded overcoat higher around her own neck. Made of dark grey cashmere and almost touching the ground, the coat had seen better days, but warmed and enfolded her in a way her late husband never had. Restarting the engine, she was glad that she would shortly be home where she and Gracie could roast in front of the fire without anyone throwing open the windows complaining about how hot it was. A jacket potato could be swiftly cooked whilst she fed Gracie, then she'd enjoy it on a tray in front of some rubbish on the TV with a large glass of wine and no one would make scathing comments about it not being a proper dinner. Perfect.

But somewhere near the top of the road, as she caught sight of the turret of Prospect House silhouetted against the sky, the thought of her lonely TV dinner suddenly began to pall. Gracie, impatient to get out of the car, huffed doggie breath in her face and gave her a quick affectionate lick. Sweet as it was to be reminded of a faithful companion who would never let her down, it wasn't quite how she'd pictured her life. She'd married Seb in a cloud of tulle and optimism, her head full of romantic hazy notions about raising a family and living happily ever after. Just six years later, Eloise felt half a century older in terms of experience and far too disillusioned to imagine ever having children of her own.

Perhaps she was being too suspicious about her new neighbour? Just because she'd been badly hurt by one utter prick didn't mean she had to remain under Seb's spell forever. Was it too late, she wondered looking across at Prospect House, to start again and offer Ross Farrell a little neighbourly hospitality rather than a cold shoulder? After all, she was only intending to ask him for coffee not to father her children, and it would certainly make life easier to be on polite terms with the man than trying to avoid him every time they met in the street.

In the bath the next morning, having convinced herself there was no harm in popping across the road to see how Ross was settling in, Eloise decided to shave her legs. It wasn't that they were particularly goaty but, for reasons best unacknowledged, she wanted to bother for the first time in ages. Shifting Gracie, who'd helped herself to the towel from the radiator to make a warm bed, Eloise dried herself and dug out some perfumed body lotion, then pulled a clinging soft grey cardigan over a full, muted tartan skirt. She left her hair loose, frowned at her face, applied the minimum amount of make-up as usual then, weakening, added some lipstick.

Downstairs, telling herself some housework was long overdue anyway, she fussed around gathering up magazines, straightening throws and plumping up cushions. Gracie's bed was given a makeover and her toy rabbit — to much doggie distress — hung out on the line to air.

Forbidding herself to do anything rash until she'd made a firm start on her design, Eloise sat at her drawing board and reasoned that it was only polite to make amends for her previous curt dismissal of Ross.

After an hour of clock-watching rather than working, she put the kettle on and spooned her favourite coffee into a cafetiere, checking, at the same time, to see if there were some clean mugs. First she would take Gracie for her usual walk and on the way back she'd casually knock at Prospect House and offer Ross a neighbourly coffee.

Satisfied that by sticking to her normal routine, no one could accuse her of going to extra trouble for Hookfield's very own bad-boy author, she put on Seb's coat and picked up Gracie's lead. Gracie — though still put out about her toy rabbit — cheered up enormously in anticipation of letting off steam across the racehorse training gallops and a chance to poke about in loamy soil and fallen leaves.

In the early days, the nervous dog hated to be parted from Eloise's side, fixing her with a desperate gaze as if the only person who had ever shown her love might walk out of her life without a moment's notice. Even now, if she suspected Eloise was about to go out without her, she would find ruses — like hiding one of her shoes — to stop her leaving the house, so it was immensely rewarding to see her now, so eager to be out and about. Tucking her sketchpad under her arm and deliberately not looking across at Prospect House, Eloise closed the door and let Gracie lead her down the front path. They were about to turn left on to the Downs when the tranquillity of the cold, crisp morning was ruptured by the sound of a car speeding up the residential road.

So much for wanting to experience a slower pace of life, she thought, watching the silver sports car send gritty hailstones into the air as it turned into the gravel drive of Prospect House.

Kym sprang from the car and Eloise was not in the least bit surprised to see that she looked just as sexy in a baggy navy-blue jogging suit — which even Eloise would think twice about wearing in public — as she did in a little black dress. This sweet, schoolgirlish Kym wore a rakish sheepskin aviator hat from which cute strands of pale blonde hair escaped to frame her beaming face. She bounced up the drive and let herself in.

As one front door slammed, Eloise was too busy dealing with warring emotions to notice another opening. Albert Villa, or Downs View, as it was now known, was a small, detached turn-of-the century property on the other side of the road which, thanks to the success of their double glazing business, had been given unexpected airs and graces by its latest owners, Brett and Debbie Dorling-Jones. The perfectly charming old house had been meticulously stripped of all character and expensively renovated. It now boasted a new synthetic slate roof, PVC window frames and bright pebble-dash. Some residents, like Nigel, admired the transformation, but to Eloise it jarred like a hybrid tea rose beside some lovely old damasks.

Frozen on the spot, as she stared at Kym's car and realised what a fool she could have made of herself, Eloise suddenly became aware of Brett Dorling-Jones reversing out of his drive. His white transit van moved at speed, travelling towards them in a wide arc before mounting the kerb and nearly flattening her and Gracie.

'Why don't you look where you're going, you stupid bitch,' Brett bellowed, from his open window.

Ignoring him, Eloise bent to comfort a trembling Gracie. It wasn't Brett punching the van into first gear and hurtling down the road at a speed that concerned her so much as the long face and shocked dark eyes looking anxiously into hers.

'Oh, sweetheart, it's okay,' she murmured, folding Gracie's dark head against her chest. 'You're all right.'

She pulled back a little, checking the frightened hound's face. Steadfast, dark eyes regarded her devotedly, bringing a lump to her throat.

'No one's going to hurt you ever again, I won't let them,' Eloise promised, casting a fleeting glance at Prospect House. 'No one's going to hurt either of us. It's you and me against the world.'

5

Kym's visit had been very pleasant indeed; all of the fun with none of the scrapping that so often sprang up between them. Yet the spectre of those arguments was sufficient to remind Ross why returning to London and sharing a flat together wasn't really an option. Rather than upset the apple cart, he'd simply have to stick it out at Prospect House alone. If he couldn't work here, where there were so few distractions, what else could he do to kick-start his creativity?

The next novel didn't even exist in his head. Usually, he was so immersed in the world of his imagination he was barely capable of noticing what was going on around him. Today, he'd leapt at the chance to escape from his desk when Kym turned up unexpectedly. But if he was being totally honest with himself, Kym wasn't the only woman who'd got him leaping about. Maybe that was the problem? Any time he got near the front of the house, he couldn't stop looking across the road for Eloise Blake. The fleeting sensation of her body pressed against his in the dark at the housewarming had left him unsatisfied and aching for more. She haunted his waking thoughts and cut a very erotic figure across his dreams.

He'd no sooner kissed Kym goodbye, when he spotted his neighbour across the road returning from an afternoon walk with her dog. The sound of Kym's car engine faded into the distance and as the peace and stillness resumed around him, Ross felt unusually isolated and began to wonder if the vacuum he now inhabited wasn't causing more problems than solutions. He watched Eloise draw closer. What was it about her? Was it because she was so different to the women he met in his literary circles, the ones who saw him as a useful means to further their own careers?

Rather than pressing either a type-script or — if only — her body on to him, his neighbour gave the impression of being keen to get away from him. Whatever the opposite of star-struck was, that was Eloise. Perhaps that's what intrigued him? Maybe if he got to know her better, maybe then she'd seem more ordinary? Someone who could even become a friend, perhaps, in this unfamiliar place where he felt so cut off from his normal social milieu. With a plan in mind, he grabbed his key and shot across the road before she could escape.

Her anxious look and the protective way she quickly pulled her dog close to her side wasn't the most encouraging start, but perhaps something else was wrong?

'Eloise? What's happened? Are you all right?' he asked, his gaze darting from her anxious face to the woods behind.

'Perfectly,' she insisted, regarding him suspiciously. 'Why wouldn't I be? This is the Downs, you know, not the setting for one of your novels. I walk here nearly every day and I've yet to come across anything nasty lurking in the woods.'

'Well, maybe I could join you next time?' he suggested. 'I still don't know where all these paths lead yet so it would be great if you could show me.'

No response. Ross tried to turn up the charm. He looked straight into her eyes — which usually worked. 'My reputation's not that bad, is it?' he pleaded. 'I promise you'll be safe. You're not still thinking that writing about evil deeds makes me a bad person, are you?'

Her colour heightened; she was blushing, that had to be a good sign. And now he was this close, she was even more gorgeous than he remembered. Those clear blue eyes in a lovely face, glossy brown hair with its russet lowlights and pale porcelain-smooth skin that made him long to run his hands across her cheeks to see if she was real.

'Right, that's enough. If you just want to poke fun at me, I'm going in.'

'What? What did I do?' He laughed, knowing he'd been caught out.

'Do I have to spell it out to you?' She hid her face as she bent to reassure her dog, soothing it with a smooth caress of its back. Lucky dog.

When she straightened up again she looked more composed, but not at all happy. 'How do you expect me to believe that you only want an innocent stroll across the Downs when your eyes are giving me another message altogether?' she asked.

'But Eloise — '

'No,' she shook her head. 'Don't try to tell me I'm mistaken because it won't work. It seems to me that if you can peddle your particular brand of gore and still face yourself in the mirror then you can probably cheat on your girlfriend without feeling in the slightest bit conscience-stricken too. *You* might be able to forget that you're in a relationship, but you've picked the wrong person if you think *I* could simply wipe that little detail from my mind.'

Ouch. Ross rubbed his jaw as she hurried up her path with her dog casting anxious looks at her. That hadn't just hurt, it was pretty damning. But perhaps Eloise Blake had done him a favour; what was the probability of changing her poor opinion of him starting from a base like that? He'd always been more interested in English than Maths, but it was clear the odds were stacked against him. Better read the writing on the wall and concentrate on writing his new novel instead.

★   ★   ★

In the following days, Eloise began to feel uneasy about her outburst. What if she'd been mistaken about his intentions? What if he'd only been trying to strike up an exchange of friendly banter? Wondering if perhaps she might have been a bit quick to judge Ross by

Seb's low standards, she forced herself to plough through two of his novels looking for evidence of his bad character. *The Cruellest Month*, with TV tie-in cover portraying the main character staring moodily into the distance, was an early work. For contrast, she'd also bought *Cold in the Earth* published just before Ross downed tools, with a sophisticated cover to reflect its author's elevated status. In understated tones of misty grey and white the cover picture was of the head of a stone angel, the eroded features lightly veiled by a covering of snow.

Anticipating an unpalatable blend of deaths, divorce and discontented mistresses, Eloise was interested to discover that in his hero, Finn, Ross had created a one-woman man whose on-off relationship with his journalist girlfriend, Cass, was both his salvation and damnation. Try as she might, Eloise couldn't match the brittle but beguiling Cass of Ross's imagination to Kym's superficial appeal but, as she reminded herself, since when did reason and libido have to correlate? After all, she would never have believed that her cold, critical husband had a frivolous side until his secretary put him in touch with it.

However, it was a puzzle she needed to put to one side while she pondered what to buy for her brother-in-law's birthday. Leaving Gracie, who was still uneasy in crowds, at home, she went into Ebbesham to do some food shopping and look round the shops. In the early days, the separation anxiety Gracie suffered had been agonising for them both. Gracie would cry terribly, not only from fear at the prospect of being left, but also with relief when Eloise returned.

At first Eloise longed to lavish the unhappy greyhound with affection but knew how important it was not to pet or cuddle her or do anything that might validate what a terrible thing it was to be alone until Gracie had learned to calm down. Even after all this time, there were days when Gracie still found it difficult to cope. Today, though, after only a brief disappointed glance in her direction and a sigh of resignation, the long black hound curled up like a comma, settled herself into her own duvet in a cosy corner of the living room and closed her eyes.

★   ★   ★

Later, with a heavy grey sky looming above the vaulted glass ceiling of the mall and the school day about to finish, Eloise decided to head home before the roads jammed with cars. Digging in her pocket for her keys as she moved towards the lifts to the car park, she only managed to unearth a lipsalve and some antique tissues. Swapping her bags, she was about to try a similar excavation on the other side when she became aware that her load was somewhat lighter than it should have been. She went through her carriers wondering if any had gone AWOL, and despite finding all present and correct, couldn't shake off the nasty feeling something was wrong. Taking a second look she realised, with a sudden surge of panic and nausea, what it was.

Miss Dior, proclaimed the sign in the window of the department store she'd just visited. Eloise was certainly missing something. Her handbag and therefore her purse, her bank cards, her diary and her keys, not to mention her lucky blue plastic Scarab beetle — which seemed to be taking an extended break from dispensing good fortune — should all have been by her side but were, more likely, being asset-stripped before their journey to the nearest bin. Was it too much to hope that some public-spirited person might have handed her bag in?

With a bit of luck — and if her Scarab beetle was ever going to do its stuff this might be a very good time — it might even still be lying where she'd left it. Think, Eloise, think! Where had she been? Of course, the shoes! The glitzy, sling backs with the kitten heels she'd tried on, wishing she had some excuse for buying them. She must have put everything she'd been carrying down then.

Turning against the tide of buggies and overexcited toddlers flowing towards the lifts, Eloise fought her way back through the department store. As she dodged past the perfume counters and towards the shoes she hoped for a first glimpse of her unassuming tan leather bag resting unnoticed on the back of a chair, willing it to be there. The closer she got the more certain she was that her instinct had been right, so it was all the more disappointing to find that her memory had played a trick on her.

Going on to numerous shops, various customer service desks and a public lavatory, she had still ended up one handbag and many of life's essentials down, and a further search of all her pockets had only yielded a loose coin. Not even enough to phone a friend. Flopping down on a bench in the now deserted centre, she stared blankly at the window of Ebbesham's once-controversial adult toy and lingerie shop — which seemed to have lost its shock factor now that everyone had got used to it — and wondered what on earth to do.

'Winter Warmer' promised the banner above a huge photo of a glamorous woman in distinctly scanty underwear. 'Not as warm as I'll be,' Eloise muttered out loud, 'by the time I've walked three and half miles uphill, broken into my own house, reassured my worried dog and cancelled all my bank cards. So keep your ridiculous get-up, it doesn't even have a handy pocket for a bus fare.'

'Why do you need a bus fare?' said a low, amused voice behind her. 'I thought you had a car. What's the problem?'

Eloise turned, knowing full well whose the voice was. Ross Farrell was making a habit of turning up when she least expected him.

'Given our last conversation, I'm surprised you're even giving me the time of day,' she remarked, quietly.

He shrugged. 'Well, I couldn't find any puppies to kick so I thought I'd come and perve at some innocent woman doing her shopping instead.'

Eloise felt a hot tide of shame wash over her, but when she dared squint up at him, he was smiling. Not that it did anything to make her feel better. In fact, looking up at his tall, masculine frame, his dark hair a little too long to be tidy, and those grey eyes — which she reckoned could brighten every morning for any fortunate woman they gazed down upon — made her even more uncomfortable. Had she jumped to all kinds of unflattering conclusions about a man she barely knew simply because he was too good-looking for her personal comfort? She buried her face in her hands, took a deep breath and came up for air. 'I can't believe how rude I was to you,' she said, squirming. 'I shouldn't have said what I did — I mean, I hardly know you. I do apologise.'

'Apology accepted,' he said, the corner of his mouth lifting in just a hint of suppressed laughter as he plonked himself down beside her. 'Now, tell me what's wrong.'

Eloise stole another quick glance at him. He looked back at her with sympathetic eyes and waited. Eloise thought about it. Hadn't Kym said right from the beginning that Ross was looking forward to doing his bit for the community? Maybe she'd been misreading him. Perhaps he saw her not as a potential conquest but as a lost cause? He'd probably decided that coming to her rescue on a regular basis was, on balance, preferable to running a stall at the church fete, or taking part in the village panto. So why protest? Why not let Ross simply take her carrier bags? They'd probably be safer in his hands, anyway. She took a deep breath, stood up and faced the inevitable.

⋆　⋆　⋆

'We can't stop,' Eloise insisted as her father tried to offer Ross a whisky, 'Ross has gone out of his way to run me over here to pick up the spare keys, and Gracie — '

'Will be fine,' David Blake assured her, looking over his rimless spectacles at her. 'Another half an hour or so won't make any difference. Thanks to you, she's a much more settled animal now than the nervous creature you took on. Just relax for five minutes, will you, before you go dashing out the door.'

Her father was slightly better at hiding his curiosity than her mother, but heaven knows they'd both had plenty of practice. Through Eloise and Cheryl — before her sister had faced the inevitable and settled down with Darren — the Blakes had been introduced to a number of strange men, some stranger than others. Nevertheless, since Ross was the first man she'd brought near them since Seb, her mother, to her credit, was demonstrating remarkable restraint.

'Nuts?'

Like everything else so far, including an overenthusiastic greeting from Wurst, her parents' miniature dachshund, Ross took Marina's comment in his stride. 'Thank you, but no.' He smiled, waving a hand, and said, 'I'm fine.'

'Crisps? Sandwich? I've got some nice ham in the fridge. I could fry you an egg to go with it?'

Wurst, lying almost on top of the flame-effect gas fire, began to whimper.

'How many times do I have to tell you?' Marina said, picking the little dog up and plonking him on a lilac throw covering the other half the sofa where Ross sat. 'If you get too close to the fire you'll get a burnt willy.'

'I shall make sure I keep my distance then,' Ross answered, gravely.

Looking delighted, Marina giggled. 'Oh you fool! I didn't mean you! As if I'd talk to you like that when we've only just been introduced. Listen, I've got some lovely chicken breasts in the fridge, why don't you two go and rescue Gracie and then come back and have some dinner with us?'

Eloise interrupted before her mother could work in a joke about her lovely breasts. 'Ross is busy. Besides, his partner might have something to say about that, Mum.'

Marina looked momentarily crest-fallen. Eloise could practically see her mind working. The little vertical furrow creasing her brow deepened. What sort of partner? She'd be wondering.

'What does your partner do then, Ross?'

Quite restrained, thought Eloise, thankful she hadn't asked Ross if his partner was a busty blonde or a bloke sporting leather trousers and a moustache.

'I can't think who Eloise's talking about,' he said, his grey eyes sparkling with amusement, 'I live alone.'

'But Kym — '

'Is my step-sister,' he grinned at Eloise. 'She's just set up her own business as an interior designer.'

6

Single. Eloise didn't dare make eye contact because she could hear the laughter in his voice. She'd been censoring all those taboo thoughts about him, attributing all sorts of evil intent to his character and going out of her way to avoid temptation and all this time he'd been single. She took a couple of deep breaths, but nothing stopped her mind racing. Perhaps he hadn't been playing with her feelings, after all? He'd even come back for more when she'd shown him nothing but mistrust. So where did she go from here? She sneaked a glance at him for a clue, only to be outmanoeuvred when he saw and winked at her.

'Kym talked me into letting her loose on Prospect House to add to her portfolio,' he went on smoothly. 'Her phone's red hot thanks to her turning my place into an arctic wilderness of white walls and cool furniture.'

'Oh, but that must feel desolate,' Marina said with a gleam in her eye, 'especially with no one to warm it up with you!'

The corner of her dad's mouth twitched. Eloise might have found it amusing too if Marina had been somebody else's mother. She needed time to think and that meant getting Ross out of there before her parents put one and one together and paired them up like two lost socks.

'I really should be off,' she said to Ross who was happily tickling Wurst, even though the wretched animal was shredding a bone right next to him.

'I was hoping to persuade Ross to join me in a proper drink,' her father piped up, clearly ready to dig in for the evening.

Eloise glared at them all. Could none of her family behave? 'Ross is driving. And Gracie might have learned to be patient, but she can't cross her legs forever. Besides, if I don't collect my car soon I'll have to remortgage to pay the parking fee.'

Everyone, it seemed to her, looked at her reproachfully. Ross nudged Wurst over and got to his feet with great reluctance. Her dad had resumed an expression of polite distance and her mother, well, her mother was looking quite angry.

'Wurst!' she bellowed. 'How could you?'

Since Ross's jacket had been lying on his throw, Wurst had clearly mistaken it for a new and grand doggie chew and had shredded two of the leather-covered buttons. Realising that his look of infinite remorse was not going to placate on this occasion, Wurst shot off under the oak sideboard where Marina, waving her slipper ineffectually, could not reach him.

'Horrid, horrid beast!' she lamented, getting to her feet.

'It's quite all right,' Ross told her. 'It's only a couple of buttons.'

'Oh it's too bad!' Marina insisted,

still clutching one slipper.

'Mum,' Eloise warned.

'Well it is too bad,' Marina said, rounding on her. 'The first decent man you've brought round here in years and now we'll never see him again.'

'Mum!' Eloise wished she could join Wurst under the sideboard.

Ross laughed. 'It's very kind of you to say so, even if Eloise doesn't agree. She thinks anyone who chooses to spend their time surrounded by rotting corpses is not to be trusted.'

'Well,' Marina went on, 'I always told her 'you'll go all round the orchard until you pick a sour bugger' and I was right! When that husband of hers — I'm sorry, what did you say about rotting corpses?'

'Calm down, Marina,' her dad interrupted. 'He doesn't mean he's Fred West. He's an author; he writes about rotting corpses. Actually, you're quite a fan of his — that TV series you watch between your fingers.'

'Noooo!' Marina gasped. 'And you'd

never think it to look at you!' She dropped the slipper she'd been wringing, giving Wurst time to slink unnoticed from under the sideboard. Treating Ross to her best coquettish look, she made a few unsubtle adjustments to her hair.

Grateful that her mother had been distracted before she could expand on the subject of her marriage, Eloise acted quickly. 'Mum, Dad, thanks for the keys. I'm sorry it's a flying visit but I really do have to get back to Gracie. Now, would one of you run me back to Ebbesham to collect my car?'

'Eloise, I'll take you wherever you need to go,' Ross said, frowning.

'But your work — '

'Really,' he insisted, 'it's no trouble.'

Eloise eyed him doubtfully. She had a feeling her troubles had only just begun.

★　★　★

Ross had been enjoying watching Eloise struggling to keep her parents in line.

Her father might have hidden his curiosity better, but there was no mistaking the look that told him to mess with Eloise's feelings at his peril. And Marina? Family gatherings certainly wouldn't be dull with her about. Yet his evening had been considerably spoilt by the mention of that word 'husband' especially in connection with Eloise as it raised all kinds of unwelcome questions.

Where was this husband, for example, and why had the Khans at the convenience store gone out of their way to tell him about his neighbour who lived on her own? At least he could hazard a guess now as to why Eloise always looked so tense and unhappy. Not that her private life was any of his business. Except that it would be nice to see her looking more relaxed and to be on the receiving end of a smile, for a change, instead of a suspicious frown. It bothered him that she was apparently willing to give the benefit of the doubt to a dodgy husband, but barely gave him the time of day.

In London, people fussed around him, hung on his every word and generally lavished him with attention. Here, Eloise simply refused to be impressed. She was courteous if distant with him whenever their paths crossed in Hookfield but, frankly, his ego was a little bruised. Meeting her parents tonight, had at least given him a clue as to why Eloise always turned away from him; she was too busy eating her heart out waiting for this husband of hers to return.

It was dark now, but as the turning for Hookfield approached, Ross still couldn't help searching his rear-view mirror for headlights to see if Eloise's car was tucked behind him. He'd hung around outside the car park making sure her old Focus was going to start, then fretted all the way up from Ebbesham about how her tyres would cope with the uphill slog over icy roads. It was a bad habit to have got into, this trying to make sure she was safe when she'd made it plain she didn't need to be looked after — at least not by him. Just because he lived in a house with a Gothic tower, he reminded himself, didn't mean he had to keep going to her rescue.

Worse still, his concerns now even extended to her greyhound. Poor Gracie must be wondering where her mistress had got to. The road was black behind him; Eloise must have been caught at the last set of lights so the unfortunate dog would have to hang on for a bit longer. Eloise's parents, on the other side of Ebbesham, were close but he was right on the doorstep. Now, if he had a spare key he could nip in and let the desperate animal out.

* * *

Gracie, relieved in more ways than one, expressed her delight at having company again by bounding up and down the front path squealing excitedly. The winter darkness made it seem later than it was, so rather than risk incurring the wrath of the Brett Dorling-Jones for waking his daughters, Eloise told herself it was plain good manners to invite Ross to step inside for a moment whilst they finished their conversation.

The minuscule lobby, a later addition to the house, was designed to screen the living room from callers at the front door who could otherwise see straight into it. With Ross pressed so close though, it seemed uncomfortably intimate. Rather reluctantly, she let him into the front room which also seemed to shrink in his presence.

'How surprising.' He smiled, taking in the room with a swift appraising gaze. 'I don't know what I expected, but it wasn't this. It's amazing, like walking into an illustration from the Arabian Nights.'

Her parents were always telling her how nice the room would look when it was finished so Eloise was secretly pleased Ross understood the effect she'd achieved on a very tight budget. In the lamplight, no one could tell how much of the gilded wood and inlaid metal picture frames winking from dimly-lit corners had been reclaimed or rescued from skips, or that the furniture had been junk shop finds.

'Not all of the distress is artificial,' she told him, running her fingers over the cracks and dents in the patchy, powdery, rose painted walls, 'but I had to make a virtue of necessity and, besides, I like this faded, ethereal feel.'

'It's enchanting,' Ross agreed, his glance resting on the large over-mantle mirror darkly reflecting the leafless trees. Eloise went over to pull the blue velvet curtains she'd wrangled for on eBay and could feel him watching her.

'You're very creative,' he told her. 'You wouldn't like to redesign Prospect House for me, would you? Maybe then the place wouldn't feel so bloody cold all the time.'

If only he knew she'd redecorated the house opposite several times over in her mind's eye. Actually, she decided, folding her arms, it was a good job he didn't know or he might think she had designs on him as well. 'I don't think that would be very diplomatic, do you? Not when your step-sister's worked so hard for you. What?' she said, seeing him trying to hide a grin.

'I can just see her face when I tell her you thought she was my significant other.' He laughed.

'It was an easy mistake to make! *I* can still see *her* face when she found me in your study at the housewarming,' Eloise shuddered. 'She didn't look very happy.'

'She thought I needed rescuing,' he explained, 'fans occasionally think they've bought a piece of me along with a book and can be a bit persistent. But now she's taking a different view, thinks I need to get out more. When she called in with some post last week, she accused me of being a recluse.'

'Oh,' Eloise said awkwardly, remembering how miffed she'd been when Kym had turned up at the very moment she'd decided to wave an olive branch at Ross. Wasn't that the real reason why she'd been so off-hand with him? 'Well, I'm glad you were out and about today or I might still be fighting my way home.'

'I've been thinking about that,' he said, his grey eyes resting on hers, making her keenly aware, suddenly, that he was the first man beyond her immediate family who'd ever been in this room. 'Are you all right for money? I can help you out with some cash until your bank cards are replaced.'

'There's no need,' she was glad to reassure him, 'the Bank of Mum and Dad gave me a temporary loan.'

He nodded and continued, 'I also wondered if it would make sense for us to swap spare keys in case of emergency. Eloise, I don't want you to think I'm prying but you know how people talk in small villages.'

'Do I?' she said, arching her eyebrows.

'Especially to incomers like me. The couple who run the convenience store were very quick to tell me about the lovely lady who lived opposite when they found out which house I'd bought.'

A lot of women would have been reassured by the wry smile he flashed at her, but Eloise could only wonder about the direction the conversation was taking.

'They mentioned that you'd been on your own ever since you've lived here,' he added.

'They did, did they?' Eloise averted her gaze from his and drew a deep breath. Just when she was starting to believe that life had moved on, that the seedy stories about Seb had faded with his memory, it seemed she was still the subject of speculation and gossip.

'They were only being neighbourly,' he added, seemingly aware of her concern. 'They're worried about you being alone here and seemed happy that I'd be around if the wheel came off. Of course, I didn't realise you were married, but if your husband's away a lot of the time then I want you to know that I'm here if you need me. The houses at this end of the road are a bit vulnerable and some people might regard a single woman as a soft target.'

No doubt it was the impact of losing her handbag which was finally catching up with her, but Eloise was starting to feel sorry for herself and could feel the sting of tears. She worked so hard to build a new life, yet the edifice was still fragile and liable to be dragged down by the old one.

'I just want to tell you,' he said, startling her as he casually reached across and took her hand, 'that if ever you're scared or you need someone at any time, don't hesitate to give me a shout. Please?'

Eloise's pulse leapt at the casual intimacy. The brush of warm fingers against her skin. 'What do you think you're doing?'

'Sorry,' he shrugged, letting go and looking as confused by what he'd done as she felt. 'It was important to know you were listening to me.'

'Oh, I heard you. There's nothing wrong with my hearing.' She'd tried to inject a note of levity into her tone, but really she was as upset with herself as she was with him. Having dragged herself up from rock bottom, she was proud of how much she'd achieved on her own. Her hopes and dreams hadn't all died with Seb; somehow she'd found the inner strength to carve out her own life and without a knight in shining armour hurrying to her rescue. Now, in a single stroke, Ross Farrell had reduced her to a quivering mess.

'I'm sorry if I sound churlish, but I think you're seeing danger where there is none. It might suit the conventions of your kind of fiction to assume that every woman on her own is ripe for attack, but I'm actually perfectly capable of looking after myself,' she said struggling to convince herself. 'Of course, I'm grateful that you happened to be there just at the right time today and for being such a help this evening, but I'm fine, really.'

Ross frowned at her. 'Are you sure you're all right?'

'Perfectly,' Eloise assured him, her words sounding falsely bright and brittle, even to her own ears. 'I'm used to looking after myself so I don't need a minder and you've done your bit for Neighbourhood Watch. Really though, there's nothing to be concerned about; I've always felt safe here. This is a village where we trust each other. Live and let live.'

'Fair enough,' Ross nodded slowly, the corners of his mouth lifting wryly as he acknowledged defeat. He moved towards the lobby and in the awkward shuffle round each other in the cramped space, there was nowhere to hide. Seeing his hurt expression, Eloise realised she might have gone a bit far. She reached out and tentatively touched his arm, the sleeve of his leather jacket cool under her hand. 'You're looking at the village as an outsider,' she continued on a conciliatory note, 'you haven't lived here long enough to get to know everyone properly, that's all.'

Gracie seemed to want to placate him too. She loped over to him and was rewarded when he moved away from Eloise and ran his hand over the animal's head and along her back with smooth, soothing strokes. You had to give him credit for persistence, Eloise thought, not content with trying to ingratiate himself with her — despite reaching the conclusion that she was a married woman — Ross Farrell was now trying to work his charms on her dog. And succeeding too, she tut-tutted to herself as Gracie closed her eyes in bliss. At the door, Ross paused for a moment.

'But I have lived here long enough for you to make your mind up about me, apparently,' he observed. 'Who do you think you know, Eloise, the author or the man?'

He strode out, leaving her to decide that she seemed to have a knack for making men disappear; it was just a pity she couldn't do something useful with it. Watching him cross the road, Eloise wasn't convinced there was much of a difference. Seb had been perfectly lovely to everyone too — apart from her — so it was entirely plausible to her that Ross Farrell's disturbingly good looks masked a troubled personality.

Seemingly aware of her gaze, he turned and Eloise quickly retreated inside before he caught her watching him. The blink of the answerphone forced her to gather her frantic thoughts, the message chasing away her immediate worries because her handbag — contrary to all her expectations — had been found under a bench by a security guard locking the shopping centre up for the night. Despite not knowing what was left of the contents, Eloise collapsed on the sofa feeling very relieved and grateful that her luck had changed. And then she heard a high-pitched scream.

7

Gracie! Eloise could taste the sharp metallic tang of her own fear as she realised that she'd been so wrapped up in her own feelings that she'd closed the door behind Ross without even noticing that the nervous greyhound was missing. Outside, Gracie's cries of distress filled the air. Running onto the Downs towards the sound, she quickly found the frightened animal guarding a narrow stretch of track where Brett Dorling-Jones — hulking and luminous in his yellow high visibility running top — was backed against a tree.

'Get your dog out of my way now,' he roared above the noise, 'or I'll kick its bleeding head off.'

'Stop shouting at her,' Eloise pleaded. 'Can't you see she's beside herself with fear? Gracie, sweetheart, it's all right.'

'No, it's not bleeding all right,' Brett

bellowed over Gracie who was still yapping hysterically and refusing to give up her territory. 'And you, you're not fit to call yourself a dog owner if you can't control it. Now call her off and let me get past.'

'Really, she won't hurt you,' Eloise insisted, moving slowly so as not to throw the scared animal into deeper panic, 'she's just very frightened. You're far more intimidating to her than she is to you, you know. Could you please stop shouting for one moment until I can make her realise she's safe?'

'Gracie, sweetheart,' she murmured softly. 'Calm down now, pet, you're fine.'

Gracie's eyes rolled wildly, pale crescents of terror flickering in her dark head, but she refrained from barking just long enough to lull Brett into a false sense of security. He stepped forwards and Gracie lunged towards him, snarling.

'If she touches me, she's dead,' Brett rasped, his laboured breathing heavy in the night air.

'Stop right where you are,' Ross ordered. Eloise almost wept with relief as his tall figure appeared beside her. 'Give the dog a chance to calm down as you've been asked.'

Brett gave a short laugh. 'And give her another opportunity to attack me? No way.'

'She hasn't attacked you,' Eloise cried.

He shook a luminous-yellow sleeve at her. 'She's dangerous and out of control — and that's what I'm telling the police first thing tomorrow.'

'And get charged with wasting police time?' Ross said calmly. 'Think about it. Think how ridiculous you're going to look when they turn up expecting to find a breed of Pit Bull Terrier then find out you're complaining about a pensioned-off greyhound with no teeth. It's just your high-vis gear setting her off; look, she's perfectly biddable.'

Eloise held her breath as he knelt down on the pitted track and called Gracie to him. It was hopeless; she was almost afraid to look. Even in the early days when the sight of any man could shred Gracie's nerves for days, she'd never seen her this terrified. Surely she was far too overwrought to respond? Assuming she was even aware of him, what chance would Ross, an unfamiliar male have, when Eloise herself couldn't reach the frightened creature?

Brett, shamed into temporary submission, remained rooted to the spot. Eloise could hear his ragged breathing quieten and prayed that he wasn't gathering himself for a fresh verbal assault. The tense ceasefire that followed seemed set to be broken by the smallest twig snapping in the silence then, suddenly, looking absolutely exhausted, Gracie simply let go of the fight. She slunk over to Ross and rested her head against his thigh. Crooning softly to her all the while, Ross placed one arm round her shoulder and another under her bottom and lifted her up.

'The door's unlocked,' Eloise said quietly, as Ross nodded towards her house. Even Brett wasn't stupid enough to move while Gracie could still see him, though he still managed to hiss, 'You haven't heard the last of this,' to Eloise as she followed after Ross.

* * *

'Where would you like her?'

'Upstairs,' Eloise answered without hesitation. 'She'll sleep pretty much anywhere she has a duvet, but she likes being at the foot of my bed best if she can get away with it. The peace and quiet will help her gather her thoughts and I can soothe her if she wakes in the night.'

Ross admired Gracie's taste. He wouldn't mind getting that close to Eloise either. Or having her to turn to in the small hours. Concentrate on that word 'husband', he reminded himself, remembering that his stock could fall just as swiftly as it had risen. Lay the dog down nice and quietly and get out before you do anything rash.

'Left at the top of the stairs,' Eloise said, following him.

Ross sucked in his breath as he found himself in Eloise's bedroom and it wasn't just the effort of carting a large greyhound up a steep flight of stairs making his heart thump, as she squeezed past him to switch on a bedside lamp. Eloise had kept the delicate, otherworldly theme going here with a softer wash of rose on the walls, clever little sketches — he recognised Gracie in one of them — in old gold frames and a wonderful antique cheval mirror shyly reflecting an ivory Victorian-style bedstead piled high with pillows in crisp white linen and an old-fashioned eiderdown.

It was soft without being sentimental or sickly, and unashamedly feminine without being girlie. Interestingly though, there was no evidence of a husband. So what was Sleeping Beauty doing all alone with her dark hair uncoiling across the pale pillows night after lonely night? If he hadn't got an armful of dog, his thoughts might have strayed to the idea of waking her with a kiss and then what? He'd be out the door in double quick time and never get another chance to spend even a few precious moments in her company ever again.

He laid the quivering greyhound gently in her bed, stroking her until she closed her eyes and the shivering subsided. He still had the chance to leave before blotting his newly clean copybook. As for those daydreams about discovering the secret of Eloise's glorious body beneath all those layers of clothes? Well, perhaps he'd have to start taking punishing walks across the Downs until he was too tired to fantasise, instead. Yes, that ought to help, he decided, straightening up to find her watching him unguardedly, her lips slightly parted and her eyes dark and seductive in the half-light.

★ ★ ★

It was Ross's frown when he glanced up at her that made Eloise snap her mouth shut. The way he was staring at her as if she was a crazy dog lady who'd lived on her own for longer than was good for her and might suddenly demand that he throw her back on the bed and make hard, hot lust to her. And he was right to be suspicious. She really was in trouble if the sight of a man gently stroking her greyhound was getting to her. What if it was Nigel next time, casually leaning in through the car window to pat Gracie on the head? Would she be able to prevent herself asking him to show her his pump? Or Brett? What if Brett stumbled across them on the Downs and, in a fit of remorse, tried to make amends? Would she drag him into the bushes and demand he take her roughly against a tree?'

'There, there, don't look so worried,' Ross said, sparing her further unpleasant thoughts and resting his hand lightly on her shoulder. Eloise tried not to squirm at his touch. It was looking at his strong hands cradling Gracie, setting her gently in her bed and deftly massaging the troubled dog's tense body that had made her imagination wander in such a lurid direction. His fingers burned through her clothes, suggesting plenty, delivering almost nothing. She wanted to tear off the restrictive fabric, grab his hand and press it against her breast.

Ross's hand dropped as if he'd just read her thoughts. 'You've had a long day,' he murmured. 'I should leave you in peace.'

Eloise was feeling anything but peaceful as she led them back downstairs. Sitting alone for what was left of the evening, turning the events of the day over and over in her head didn't hold any appeal.

'Ross, don't go.'

His expression was quizzical, making her blush like an idiot.

'I don't know about you,' she said, laughing and trying to sound casual, 'but I could do with a glass of wine after that. And something to soak it up.

Would you like to join me? It'll only be pasta, I'm afraid, nothing very grand — '

She had to take a deep breath because everything had come out in a rush, and why the heck would he want supper with someone who'd done nothing but give him a hard time? Even so, she hoped he would appreciate her conciliatory gesture and see it for what it was; an attempt to put them on a more neighbourly footing. The sudden rush of blood to her nether regions up in her bedroom must have been a kind of erotic swooning at being bowled over by his heroic behaviour. And as for her stomach flipping when the corners of his mouth lifted in a smile, it probably had more to do with hunger than desire. Nothing that a wodge of carbohydrate and a glass of wine wouldn't put right.

'I thought you'd never ask.' He smiled, the smoke-grey eyes smouldering at her. 'But haven't you had enough for one day? You're a handbag down and you've had a very unpleasant encounter with that idiot Brett.'

'Gracie's unharmed though, that's the main thing, and I've still got the where-withal to rustle up a couple of bowls of tortellini,' she told him, starting towards the kitchen, 'there's better news about my bag, too, I think. I'll tell you about it.'

The kitchen was small, and accessed through the dining room. Ross followed her, but she headed him off before he could stand in her way, making her forget where everything was.

'You can sit here and talk to me through the archway while I cook,' she told him fetching a bottle of wine and a couple of glasses. Eloise liked the lambent glow of candlelight, even when she was alone, and always kept a plain metal candelabrum on the pale oak dining table. She lit the candles now and put some music on low, just to cover any awkward silences.

For a hastily thrown-together meal, it hadn't been too bad, she decided a little later. Forgetting herself, she chased a baby salad leaf slicked in French dressing round a large blue and white bowl with her fingers and popped it in her mouth. She heard Ross swallow and darted a look at him to find him studying her across the table.

'It makes a change to see you drop that guard,' he told her, his low voice husky. 'I'm so glad you asked me to join you for a meal.'

Her heart gave a fluttery leap. She sat back from the candlelight to hide her face in the shadows. The cover meant she could watch him at her leisure, giving her the opportunity to study the sharp planes of his cheekbones as he leaned towards her, close enough to expose the gleam of a handful of silver threads amongst the dark unruly curls. But when one of his strong hands stretched across the table to trace her fingers wrapped around the stem of her wine glass, it was harder to hide the bolt of excitement that shot through her.

'It can't be easy for you,' he rubbed his thumb gently across the back of her hand. 'I don't want to tread on anyone's toes, Eloise, but I meant what I said about being here if you need me. Maybe I've got this all wrong; your mother mentioned your husband but he keeps a low profile and you don't seem to have a single photo of him on display. My guess is that he's let you down somewhere along the line. I'm not trying to fill his shoes or get in the way, I'm just offering my help if your husband won't.'

'Can't,' Eloise corrected him, closing her eyes. 'He's dead.'

'Ah,' Ross, sounding embarrassed, quickly removed his hand from hers. 'I'm sorry. That would explain things.'

'Would it?' she shot him a look. 'What sort of things?'

He shoved his hand through his hair, seemingly lost for words. 'When?' he asked, at last. 'When did he . . . pass away?'

Eloise gave a snort of disbelief. 'You think there's a grieving process and timetable of appropriate responses, do you? First year: handle with care, mourner prone to fits of uncontrollable crying or anger, especially on the anniversary of all those tricky little 'firsts'. First birthday alone? First Christmas alone? First mortgage application, just me, all by myself?' She buried her face in her hands, trying to breathe deeply before she lost control completely.

She heard Ross push his chair away from the table and get to his feet. 'I'd better go. I didn't *think* anything or want to suggest that there's any kind of schedule for emotions. Of course, I don't believe that. I just didn't *think*. I'm sorry. Eloise?'

She could feel him standing over her, but just couldn't look up because of the effort it was taking to hold back the tears and stop her bottom lip from quivering.

'Eloise?' he repeated softly. 'I truly didn't mean to open up old wounds. I wouldn't have hurt you for the world. I'm not implying you can ever recover from a loss like that. It must be devastating to have to carry on without the person you love so much.'

She tried to speak, but her throat was so constricted it came out as a croak.

'Sorry?' He pulled up a chair and sat next to her, stroking her shoulders. 'I'm sorry; I didn't catch what you said. Get your breath back while I make you a cup of tea.'

Eloise shook her head fiercely and grabbed hold of his hand to stop him moving away. 'I didn't.'

Ross tilted his head and frowned, clearly trying to make sense of what she was telling him.

She let go of him and folded her hands in her lap. 'I didn't love my husband.'

What a relief it was, at last, to say it out loud. 'I did, at first. Of course I did or I wouldn't have married him. I thought I loved him because 'love' was a convenient label for the impact he had on my life. That sudden sense of need. I thought what I was feeling was the most you could feel for someone. It wasn't love, though, just infatuation; a poor, feeble impression trying its best to be love, but too thin, too inadequate to weather any storm. Whatever it was, it had certainly died by the time they cut him out of his wrecked BMW with his latest girlfriend at his side.'

She saw Ross wince.

'I didn't *want* him to die; no one deserves that. But he destroyed every chance we ever had of making our relationship work. Whatever I gave him, he threw away. Nothing I did ever pleased him and in the end all I wanted was to feel like myself again; to be free from the bullying, the belittling, the uncertainty of wondering what sort of mood he'd be in when he finally decided to come home.

'When that knock on the door came in the middle of the night and I opened it to find the police standing there, all I could think was that I'd made it happen. That I had somehow been responsible for his death. At least his girlfriend escaped with superficial cuts and bruises, though she might be more circumspect, next time, about getting in the car with a drunk. But if only I'd found the courage to stand up to him, to make him face up to his problems instead of wishing every waking hour that he would just disappear, maybe he'd still be alive?'

8

The next morning, Eloise was roused by a persistent blast of gnawed bone and doggie chew wafting across her pillow. Wrinkling her nose in disgust, she came to in a hurry when she opened her eyes and found Gracie kneeling over her, peering into her face and uttering little huffs of distress.

'Gracie?' she began, wondering why the greyhound was so keen to wake her up in what still felt like the middle of the night. Except it wasn't moonlight filtering through the gap in the curtains, but a clear, watery sunshine. Glancing at her bedside clock, she saw that after the emotional rollercoaster of the previous day, she had overslept. Suddenly the horror of blurting everything out to Ross came back to her and she flopped back on the pillows, staring at the ceiling in mortification.

A huge, emotional splurge might have given her some temporary relief after three years of withholding her true feelings about Seb, even from her own family, but would Ross ever be able to look her in the eye again? Was that really the way to thank him for rescuing Gracie from Brett Dorling-Jones? No wonder he'd behaved as if she was as overstrung as her nervous dog.

She felt like retreating back under the duvet as she thought about the awkward moment in her lobby as he'd been about to leave. Her eyes closed as she recalled leaning back against the wall so he could get past. Instead though, he paused in front of her and she found herself looking up to him, meeting his gaze. After what felt like an eternity, he reached out and gently cupped her head. The breath she'd been holding shuddered through her as his fingers trailed through her hair and he pulled her towards him. She buried her groan in his chest, overwhelmed by how good it felt to be held again, to draw strength from him, the warmth of his strong body, his clean masculine smell . . . and then he'd dropped a gentle kiss on the top of her head and told her to get some rest, treating her with all the care and respect anyone would accord a crazy lady who'd been living with her dog far too long.

Oh lord, poor Gracie! While she was lying there eating her heart out about scaring her neighbour away, Gracie must, once again, be bursting to be let out. She threw back the cover becoming aware, at the same time, of a commotion under her window as someone beat a tattoo on her front door. As she sat there trying to make sense of the noises, Gracie tried to help by offering her a choice of footwear.

Staggering downstairs in an unconventional slipper and flip-flop combo, Eloise reflected that being single and free to wear whatever she liked to bed had its advantages. Instead of slinky, slithery nighties which slipped off her shoulders or got tangled up in her legs, she could slob around in ancient T-shirts and granny bed-socks if she wanted. She could slather her face with lotions and potions without anyone complaining about the smell and read all night long if she liked.

Unfettered by anyone else's opinion, she had not descended into total anarchy, but had developed a rather surprising taste for virginal white cotton gowns with pin-tucked bodices and little pearl buttons. Most importantly, she was perfectly decent for facing whoever was out there. Seb, no doubt, would have passed some withering comment if he'd been able to see her. But unless his spirit had taken possession of something far more substantial, he wasn't the one she was about to take to task for hammering her door down.

A young woman with practical short blonde hair and a capable expression was standing outside. She wore a sensible green fleece and the kind of waterproof trousers and strong boots that seemed to indicate she was probably one of the rangers who regularly patrolled the Downs. They were supposed to look out for antisocial miscreants, but clearly missed Brett Dorling-Jones every time.

'Miss Blake?'

Gracie, beside her, sighed and settled herself at Eloise's feet evidently deciding that this was going to be a longer exchange than Eloise herself anticipated.

'I'm Amy Merry. Animal Warden for Ebbesham Borough Council.' She waved a plastic ID card on the end of a green lanyard. 'Our call centre received a complaint this morning from a concerned member of the public about a dangerous dog. I wondered if you knew anything about the matter.'

'Sorry,' said Eloise, shrugging, 'it wasn't me. I haven't put in a complaint. Are you sure you've come to the right address. Who are you looking for?'

Amy Merry squared her shoulders. Eloise thought she could probably be quite intimidating in the right circumstances. She certainly didn't live up to her name.

'The caller chose to remain anonymous. But the complaint, Miss Blake, was about you. Could you please confirm for me just how many dogs you keep at this address?'

Brett. Bloody Brett Dorling-Jones. Eloise bit her tongue and concentrated on looking innocent.

'Just Gracie, here. My greyhound and as you can see, her favourite occupation is sleeping. Attacking anyone would use up far too much of her energy.'

'Miss Blake, I'm afraid as far as the law is concerned, dogs don't actually have to physically attack someone for the police to take action. It's a criminal offence for any dog — regardless of what breed it is — to be dangerously out of control in a public space. And that means any occasion where a bystander is afraid for their own safety. Prosecution could lead to a substantial fine or a prison sentence.'

Eloise could feel herself grow pale. 'And Gracie? What would that mean for her?'

'In the event of a dog causing actual injury, there is an automatic presumption that it would be destroyed — unless you could convince the court that the animal wasn't a danger to the public.'

Gracie, exhausted with the additional duty of having to wake Eloise up, twitched in her sleep. The thought of the gentle, trusting dog being put down because of her own moment of irresponsibility made Eloise's eyes mist over. But, presumably, if Brett really thought he could prove that Gracie was all that dangerous, he would have gone straight to the police rather than the local authority.

'Miss Merry,' she reasoned, 'surely it's obvious that my dog wouldn't harm a fly? As it happens, she's quite scared of flies, too. She hides her face in her duvet if one tries to bother her. It sounds to me as if someone's made a purely malicious complaint to frighten *me*.'

There was a flash of sympathy in the young woman's eyes, suggesting that she wasn't without compassion. 'I agree that she looks very docile at the moment, but in the same way as people, dogs have different likes and dislikes. Especially rescue dogs, some of them can be quite phobic say, for example, about men . . . '

Eloise shut her eyes as a door slammed across the road, then opened them a fraction when she heard footsteps on gravel. Whilst she would have preferred Ross not to see her with her face pink and shiny from sleep, making her feel about as alluring as a slice of pre-packed ham, she nevertheless waved enthusiastically. Ross, with a quick glance over his shoulder presumably to see if he could pretend the greeting was intended for anyone else and escape, had no choice but to cross the road, his dark hair lifting in a slight breeze as he moved towards them.

Gracie sprung to her feet and the animal warden narrowed her eyes at her, obviously looking to see if she was about to tear Ross's throat out. Ross squatted to make of fuss of Gracie who whined softly and took advantage of his proximity to give him a sneaky affectionate lick.

'Pretty dangerous, huh?' Eloise couldn't help but remark to her official visitor.

'I've told you not to talk about me like that,' Ross grinned, almost blowing Amy Merry off her feet with his gale-force smile. 'Is there a problem?'

Eloise started to explain, but the animal warden was no longer paying attention. She was staring at Ross, a deep frown creasing her brow. As enlightenment dawned, her puzzlement transformed through several stages of belief and disbelief until she was convinced and ready to test her theory.

'You're Ross Farrell!'

Ross gave her a sweet, self-effacing grin — he did it surprisingly well, thought Eloise, given those rather brooding features. 'I am, yes.'

'Oh. My. God. I can't believe I'm talking to you. I am *such* a fan of yours!'

That fitted; anyone who took gentle

dogs away from loving homes without flinching was probably up for a bit of mindless slaughter. The dog warden was busily rummaging in her bag, 'I'm just trying to find something non-official for you to write on,' she explained sheepishly. 'I wonder if you'd mind giving me your autograph.'

'I'm not exactly a celebrity — ' Ross began, looking away. He froze for a split-second, then his gaze snapped back to Eloise and she knew immediately that something was very wrong. Fortunately, Amy Merry was too busy looking in her bag to notice.

'I've got a pen, obviously, but would you believe it, I just can't — '

'Don't worry about it,' Ross said quickly. 'Look, it's not often I get to meet a real fan, well, not unless it's at an event arranged by my publisher. I think I can do better than a scribbled signature on a scrap of paper. Why don't you pop across the road with me and choose which book you'd like me to sign for you instead? A little 'thank you' for the support? Eloise — you must be freezing in that, erm, nightie-thing. You should get inside and warm up.'

'But there's a procedure I have to follow,' Amy Merry insisted, looking mulishly determined.

'Even if I act as a character witness for Miss Blake *and* her dog?' Ross said winningly. 'I promise I'll see to it they both behave.'

For a moment the animal warden seemed to take root, then she reached in her bag and shoved a leaflet at Eloise. 'Read this carefully, please, and take notice. If I hear there's been any more trouble, there won't be another warning. Next time it'll be a police matter.'

'Go in,' Ross urged, taking Amy Merry's arm and steering her away. 'And shut your door before you catch a cold.'

Eloise was dimly aware of feet pounding closer. She shut the door and rushed to the window just in time to see

Brett Dorling-Jones almost careering into the animal warden who would have gone flying if Ross hadn't been holding on to her arm in a tight grip. She looked down at Gracie who tilted her head on one side and gave her a doggie grin. 'I don't believe it,' Eloise told her, 'Ross Farrell has saved us, yet again.'

⋆ ⋆ ⋆

Ross chuckled when, shortly after the warden left — and for a while he thought she was all set to move in with him — he opened his door to find Eloise and Gracie standing there looking at him expectantly. He invited them in and instantly the white vacuum that was his hall was filled with life and warmth.

'We were just going for a walk,' Eloise explained rather unnecessarily since she was well wrapped up in her oversized charcoal coat, her serious blue eyes peeping out from a floppy Fair Isle patterned beret. 'So we won't disturb you.'

'You're not disturbing me.' He smiled. At least no more than she had this morning, standing there in that deceptively modest white nightgown with her long, dark hair falling in wanton contrast around her shoulders. When she stretched her arms to make a point and the sheer fabric tightened across her breasts, it had been a struggle not to stare. She had no idea of how sexy she looked — rather the opposite, in fact, as if she was deliberately trying to swamp her curves in swathes of fabric.

He thought he understood her a little better after her revelation of the previous evening. Even the way she dressed, shrouding her lovely figure in layers of clothes, might be interpreted as self-defence, protecting herself in a clothing cocoon. That philandering husband of hers had damaged her self-esteem and left her almost as suspicious of strange men as Gracie. How tempting it had been, standing so close to her last night, to bend his lips to hers and explore that sweet mouth. To slide his hands down her back, pulling her into him to feel those soft curves pressed against his hard body. Yet, he'd resisted, because after everything she'd told him he had to prove to her he was a better man than her husband, someone who didn't carelessly take his pleasure where he found it. Had he imagined it though, when he thought he'd seen disappointment in her eyes?

'Tea? Coffee?' Anything to make her stay a little longer. 'Something for you, Gracie?'

The greyhound waved her tail at him and opened her mouth in what looked like an enthusiastic smile.

'Nothing for either of us, thank you,' Eloise replied. 'We just dropped by to give you these for everything you've done.'

From her bag, she produced a gift bag containing a bottle of wine, but he would never have guessed what was in the square package wrapped in purple tissue paper and bound with green raffia ribbon.

'It's Prospect House,' he said delightedly, looking at the small sketch set in a gilt frame. 'This is your work, isn't it?'

She nodded, her face turning pink. 'I did it before you moved in,' she told him anxiously. 'I haven't been spying on you.'

'I can tell from the size of the brambles and the overgrown garden.' He laughed. 'It's utterly delightful. Amazing. I feel really privileged, thank you!'

And seeing her eager, upturned face watching him with joy and relief, it was the easiest thing in the world to wrap his free arm round her shoulders and draw her towards him. He'd only meant to brush her lips with his, but as soon as their mouths touched, it was like coming home. He'd found the sweet spot where he was supposed to be; it was warm, welcoming, soft and sensual. Ross couldn't remember if so gentle a kiss had ever left him shaken to the core.

He paused just long enough to make sure that she was with him and the almost imperceptible movement, as she lifted her face and nudged closer towards him, ignited a flame of excitement that flared up inside him like never before. He bent his head to hers once more, saw her lips part as she lifted her head to meet him and felt her hands move up over his chest, circling his neck as their kiss deepened. He pulled her silly hat off, so that he could plunge a hand through the silky thickness of her hair, and flung it across the hall, which prompted Gracie to have a mad moment — probably, he cursed to himself, thinking it was a rabbit.

Eloise broke away from him, laughing and fanning her pink face. 'I'm in danger of bursting into flames here!' she complained, undoing the top button of her coat.

'Take something off,' he urged, evilly, 'and don't stop until you're sure you've cooled down.'

She giggled, breathless, lips full and lush with kissing and her eyes flashing with laughter. He didn't think he'd ever wanted a woman so much.

'Oh,' she said, shyly, once she'd got her breath back, 'well that was quite a thank you kiss.'

'I'm very grateful.' He smiled, pulling her close again. 'Let me show you how grateful I can be.'

She shook her head, but her eyes danced with a merriment that made him feel warm inside.

'Seriously,' he said, running his fingers down the side of her face, 'you're not offended, are you? I've been longing to do that, but it was never the right time.'

'It isn't the right time now.' She laughed as Gracie squeezed herself in between them, clutching Eloise's hat in her mouth. 'This one needs a walk and you've got work to do.'

She took her hat and clamped it on her head lopsidedly, so that he couldn't resist straightening it.

'You haven't answered my question . . . have I upset you?'

'Do I look upset?'

She was beaming at him and his heart skipped like a teenager in love.

'And now we're going, aren't we, Gracie?' she said, picking up the lead. 'We only came to thank you.'

Ross saw his opportunity. 'I think you still owe me.'

Eloise frowned, looking slightly unsure and he felt sorry for causing her any anxiety. He took her hand and patted it gently. 'I have to attend a function and I'd be honoured if you'd come with me as my guest. Trust me, I wouldn't ask you to somewhere you'd feel uncomfortable, but I think you'd enjoy it and it would mean a lot to me if you were there. Please, Eloise, it's important to me. Say you'll come.'

9

Eloise hoped that, by dropping her news into the conversation when Cheryl's mouth was full of the Danish pastry she'd bought to distract her with, somehow her sister wouldn't hear what she was saying. She brushed as much of the spray of crumbs off her dark skirt as she could and dabbed at the coffee with a tissue. Maybe it hadn't been such great timing after all, not least because Cheryl's button nose was almost quivering with curiosity.

'Don't,' she said, as Cheryl offered the last of the pastry to Gracie. 'It's not good for her teeth.'

'Oh, a little of what-you-fancy won't hurt her. Or you.' Cheryl chuckled, wiping her hands while Gracie hoovered bits off the shop floor. 'You might get a little bit of Ross Farrell, if you play your cards right. If you're very lucky, you might get a big bit of Ross Farrell — ooh, and you can get me that signed book for Darren just in time for his birthday. Well, well, well — you've kept that under your hat. So you're going on a date with your luscious neighbour? How did you manage that?'

Eloise fought the urge to tug her sister's hair or give her a pinch to shut her up the way she sometimes had when they were little.

'It's not a date. I'm simply accompanying him to a dinner for a charity he supports,' she said, stiffly.

'Uhuh.' Cheryl nodded. 'So Ross Farrell's making a shameless attempt to persuade you that he's not all bad, is he? He must be keen to impress you. So, what's the charity? Hug a Crime Writer? Ross Farrell Rehabilitation UK? The charity that likes you to say 'yes!''

Eloise scowled at her. 'The charity helps families who have a child with a life-threatening or terminal illness by providing respite care and supported holidays. Ross is a patron; he says this event's the night of the year when the trust thanks the volunteers who do all the real work, the people whose help they rely on.'

'Dying children?' Cheryl said, looking misty-eyed, 'Gosh, he really is keen to change your opinion of him.'

'He's a long-standing patron, nothing to do with me.' Eloise felt indignant on his behalf. 'It's one of the reasons he came house-hunting in this direction. He knew the area as the charity's head office is based here.'

'So tell me, El, if Ross Farrell had asked you out to a fancy restaurant or a literary awards ceremony, would you have accepted?'

Eloise stuck out her hand for her sister's plate and picked up their mugs. 'He didn't though, did he? I'm just there to help fly the flag for a good cause. Right, are we going to change the window display?'

'Oh we certainly are,' Cheryl said, with a determined gleam in her eye.

'My sister is not accompanying Ross Farrell to his charity event looking like a bag lady. I'm shutting up and we're going shopping.'

Just after the starter, Eloise sent silent thanks to her sister for being such an insistent fairy godmother. She'd walked Gracie on numerous occasions past the modern grandstand that stood, in sleek white render and glass-panelled magnificence, overlooking Ebbesham's historic racetrack and dismissed it as an overbearing imposter lacking in soul, a poor substitute for the humble old building which had previously stood there. When she'd learned from Ross that the function they were to attend was being held there, her first thought was that it wouldn't be too far to walk home if she needed to get away in a hurry. Now, in the plush comfort of one of the conference rooms, she reflected that if she hadn't listened to Cheryl she might have had to do just that.

Imagining herself turning up to this smart black tie event in her reliable old red dress, in contrast to so many beautiful women draped in gorgeous evening gowns, made her face feel quite hot. At least there was no danger of the woman in the nude-coloured gown sitting opposite overheating. The little fabric making up the top of her dress was working so hard to cover such a lot of bosom, that Eloise half-expected a nipple or two to make an uninvited appearance in someone's dinner at any moment. It was a huge compliment to Cheryl's hard work, therefore, that Ross seemed to be the only man not making mental bets on which filly would nose past the post first, but was concentrating entirely on her.

Cheryl had managed to persuade her into a clear pink ankle-length gown flatteringly cinched in at the waist to show off her curves. Eloise had baulked at its sheer bodice, but, as Cheryl pointed out, the silk slip lining made it almost demure. Ideally, Eloise would have liked to have added a few more layers; a comforting cardigan or a pashmina so as not to feel too exposed. But then she wouldn't have been sitting there feeling like the luckiest girl in the world because Ross, so handsome in his formal black suit and crisp white shirt, was at her side, one arm draped over the back of her chair, the other tracing the soft inside of her arm with his warm fingers.

Later, when Ross made his way to a rostrum to present one of the charity's most long-serving volunteers with a special award for her efforts, she could see from the reaction as he moved through the crowd that he was well-known and well-liked. Men cheered him or patted him affectionately as he passed, women smiled up at him or glanced his cheek with hurried kisses and she began to feel ashamed of her initial aversion to him and how quick she'd been to look only for the bad in his character. He was good at his job, a talented writer, and she'd allowed herself to be misled into thinking that the dark chapters of his work were a reflection of the man.

As he stood in the spotlight patiently posing for photographs with the volunteers, she took advantage of the opportunity to unashamedly ogle him. His features were stern, forbidding even, yet when he smiled it came straight from the heart. His eyes lit up with genuine warmth as an elderly lady demanded a kiss, then fished a copy of his latest book from her bag for him to sign. He was sensitive and kind with a recently bereaved young couple, who had run their first marathon together in memory of the child they'd lost and raised a huge sum for the charity in the process.

Eloise sat there reflecting that ever since Ross Farrell had moved into Prospect House, he'd gone out of his way to treat her with consideration and kindness. Whenever she'd been in difficulty, he'd seemed to sense it and come to her rescue. And, yes of course, she was quick to tell herself, she could have sorted the problem out on every occasion, because she was perfectly capable of looking after herself. And yet . . . and yet . . . just because she could soldier on alone, it didn't mean she had to. Ross Farrell was single, sexy and kind; a good man.

Once, she had blamed Seb for ruining her life, but now she understood what her parents and sister were so anxious to make her see. All the time she was hiding away, afraid to let herself feel emotions, she would ruin it for herself. Even Gracie would leave her one day, but that didn't mean she could love the rescue greyhound with anything less than her whole heart. Was it time to take a chance? At that point, Ross looked across the room for her and when he caught her eye and smiled, she was in no doubt about the answer.

'Why this particular cause?' she asked when the speeches were over and music began to play in the adjoining room. Ross poured her a glass of white wine while people drifted away to dance. He loosened his tie, looking so sexy that Eloise almost forgot she'd asked him a question and nearly used the ends to pull him towards her instead. But this was important, she reminded herself, waiting while he took a sip of his own drink.

'Ah,' he said, with a wry glance. 'I suppose you could say that being patron of this charity has helped me work through my own demons. My little sister, who was three years younger than me, was born with a serious disease which severely affected her lungs. My parents knew there was no cure, but for a few years at least, it seemed as if Sally's illness was containable. Of course, every time she was admitted to hospital, I could see their fear. The strain was written across their faces but they struggled to contain their emotions. When Sally was well they pretended to be normal mainly for my sake, because I was so young. Then one day Sally succumbed to an infection and with her death, the whole edifice crumbled and their marriage fell apart.'

'I'm so sorry,' Eloise placed her hand over his. 'How old were you?'

'I was nine. And, at the time, all I could think was how relieved I was to be away from the children's wards, away from seeing Sally struggling for breath and other families devastated by grief when their children didn't make it.'

No wonder his work was so dark. All those years of sickness, death and soaking up his parents' pain must have been absorbed and reworked into those bleak stories.

'My dad moved abroad, wanted to get away as far as possible so it's been a struggle to stay in touch with him since then. But when my mother met Kym's father at work there was a happy ending of sorts; Mum found someone strong enough to carry her through her grief, I acquired a surrogate baby sister in Kym and somehow we muddled together, became a family and lived happily thereafter.'

'They must be very proud of you and

what you've achieved,' Eloise told him, holding his gaze as he turned his grey eyes with their black velvet depths to hers. 'Success, prosperity, a lovely home, the respect of your peers and professional acclaim ... Why are you frowning?'

He shook his head and smiled. 'I just wondered how long the professional acclaim will last when I haven't written a word in two years? Maybe you've hit the nail on the head? Maybe my career took off too easily? Maybe there's no challenge any more. Nothing left for me to prove? And there's something else missing from your very generous list,' he added, taking her hand and lifting her gently to her feet.

'Oh?'

His hand was warm on the small of her back through the filmy fabric as he pulled her closer, his eyes were smoky with desire and his lips were tantalisingly within reach.

'What?' she insisted, unable to resist winding a finger between the concealed buttons of his shirt, to touch the firm muscles of his chest.

'Love, Eloise,' he said, softly, before he kissed her.

'Ross! Stop monopolising that woman and bring her to the dance floor, will you?' Someone laughed in passing, raising a glass to them both when they looked up in surprise.

'Dance?' Eloise gulped. 'Do we have to? I can't remember when I last hit a dance floor.'

'I bet there are one or two things you thought you'd forgotten how to do, but I can assure you, you will pick them up very quickly, especially,' he said, close to her ear, 'when I'm here to help you remember.'

He hadn't been wrong about the dancing, she decided a little later, and besides, the atmosphere was so upbeat and everyone was having such a good time that she forgot to be inhibited. Even when Ross left her for a moment to fetch them both a drink, she was happy on the edge of a group, swaying her hips and moving her arms. And, oh goodness, she'd even got a pull.

She grinned good-naturedly at the man in front of her. Fair-haired, very fit, as if he worked out a lot. Flattering really, and after all he wasn't doing any harm, keeping his distance and shuffling his feet. Ross would be back at any minute.

'It's Eloise, isn't it? Eloise Nichols?'

She stopped dancing and stared at him.

'Blake,' she forced out through dry lips.

'Ah.' He nodded sympathetically. 'I can see why you'd want to change your name. You look so much better, I hardly recognised you at first. You look five years younger than back then, not three years older.'

Recollection came with her heart sending her blood so fast and so loudly round her body, the pounding almost drowned out every other sound in the room.

'Stephanie Turner's husband.'

'Ex,' he acknowledged ruefully. 'Finding out she'd been shagging your husband didn't exactly do wonders for our marriage. If he hadn't wrapped his car round a tree and killed himself, I might have been tempted to do it for him.'

Eloise looked nervously about her, half-anticipating a sea of recriminatory glances, but no one had even noticed they were so busy dancing and enjoying themselves.

'I didn't come over to cause trouble,' he said, catching her expression, 'that's why I waited until your bloke was out the way. I divorced Steph, met someone new and was able to start again.' He turned and waved to a pretty blonde, who was watching them anxiously. 'Fresh start for both of us — my wife lost a child before she met me, which is why we try to help this charity and why we're here tonight. But I always wondered what happened to you, after what that shithouse of husband did to you. I'm just delighted to see you looking so well and happy. Your bloke's coming back so I'll make myself scarce, but I'm glad you've found a good'un this time.'

'You look so beautiful that I can't even leave you alone for five minutes without someone trying to steal you away.' Ross grinned, handing her a glass of cool, sparkling water. 'I'm lucky you're still here, good-looking man like that. He seemed to have a lot to say.'

'He thought I was someone he used to know,' she explained, feeling the burden of the past slip away, 'but I'm not.'

All this time she'd behaved as if part of her had died with Seb. Or if not died, retreated so deep within herself that she'd refused to feel. But that had changed the night she'd taken liberties with her housewarming invite and stumbled in the dark into Ross's arms. It occurred to Eloise that she hovered on the brink of two worlds. She could choose to stay in the past, forever reliving the terrible moment when the news of her husband's death revealed his latest betrayal of her. The last in a long line of broken promises. If she took that path, there would be no new hurts, no more heartbreak, no love, no babies and no one to come home to. Or she could take a leap into the unknown.

★ ★ ★

As it happened, Ross had been quite wrong about her remembering lost skills. Waking up in his warm embrace the next morning, she knew for certain that she was in unchartered territory. Even during the first year of her marriage, before she realised that, for Seb, the thrill of sex was in the chase, every act of love left her feeling lonelier and more puzzled than the last. But with Ross, she had experienced the bliss of a shared journey and mutual fulfilment.

It had started in her living room, beginning with a slow, sensual kiss that had her squirming against the wall. He slipped off his dinner jacket and she'd helpfully removed his tie for him and unbuttoned his shirt. He pushed his fingers through her hair and gently pulled her closer to deepen the kiss, whilst his other hand slid under the silky fabric of her dress so that he could run his fingers over her thigh, slowly upwards . . .

'Stockings,' he murmured huskily, 'wow.'

Gracie, lifting her head from her duvet where she'd settled after greeting them, sighed dramatically, which made them laugh and broke the rising tension somewhat.

'We'll go upstairs, shall we?' Eloise giggled.

'As soon as you like,' Ross had agreed, taking her hand.

And that had been the start of an unforgettable night of wonderful revelations, passionate exchanges and tender conversations. Now, through a gap in the curtains, the sunshine falling across the bed showed the first promise of spring and, with it, a suggestion of thrusting shoots and swollen buds bursting into life. Curled against Ross, who was in a drowsy state between sleep and wakefulness, she could feel another promising swelling as his erection sprang to attention. He gave a low growl as she wriggled against him and got his own back by cupping her breast and stroking her nipple, sending her instantly into a frenzy of desire. Until Gracie, who had sneaked back into the room in the middle of the night, wriggled up the bed and stuck her face in theirs.

'Woah,' said Ross, falling back on the pillow, 'I've got to tell you, dog, that your early morning breath is a humdinger.'

'I should probably do the decent thing and let her out,' Eloise sighed, sitting up. 'She's probably longing for a walk too.'

'We'll go together,' Ross said, propping himself up on the pillow next to her and watching her with dark eyes sparkling with mischief. 'After what I learned last night, you can show me some more places I haven't explored before. Outdoors, that is. We can wear Gracie out then come back to bed and get to know each other all over again.'

Eloise shook her head and slumped back down. 'I'd love to but I can't. It's my brother-in-law's birthday so we're all going over to Mum and Dad's for Sunday lunch.'

Life was so unfair; her family were always nagging her to get out and find a new man, but now she'd done what they'd asked, what she really wanted to do was stay in with him.

He nodded and said, 'It sounds fun.'

Eloise rolled her eyes at him, 'I'm surprised you can say that having met them.'

'I liked them.'

There was an option, but sitting down to Sunday lunch with her entire family goggling at Ross and asking all sorts of intrusive questions was one that could wait for another day. 'I'd invite you but it's a bit short notice.'

'And a bit too soon?' he added with a rueful smile.

He dropped a kiss on her head and rolled back the duvet to get up. Eloise folded her arms, disappointed that the spell had been broken by real life crashing in on them. It was true that, at this stage, she'd rather keep Ross to herself than share him with her overwhelming family, but it would have been nice if he'd put up more of a fight to be included. She felt better when he glanced over his shoulder at her and turned to give her a reassuring hug.

'Hey,' he said, 'don't look so worried. There'll be plenty of time to play catch up. Besides, I need to get my breath back after last night — which was fantastic, by the way. When are you due at your parents?'

She shrugged. 'One-ish.'

'That gives you two hours to lose that post-coital glow before your mum sees you.' He grinned. 'And don't forget to say hello to her for me.'

10

As dusk fell and his desk was cloaked in shadow, Ross searched in vain for a glimmer of light in the end terrace house opposite, but Eloise still wasn't home. He realised how alert he'd become to her comings and goings, seeing her and Gracie passing on their twice daily walks. Just a quick glimpse of Eloise, bundled up to face the cold with Gracie watching her adoringly, brightened his day. But today, after waking up in the sanctuary of her bed to find her spooned against him, her pert bottom settled into his lap — even with Gracie snoozing at the foot of the bed — the cruel day had felt especially long without her.

He checked his watch for the umpteenth time and went to the front door just in case he'd missed her car returning, shivering as the cold air surged towards him. He peered hopefully towards Eloise's jewel-box of a living room, hoping to see her switching on low lamps to cast soft pools of light over deep rose walls. Or, from the hearth, to see a fire catch, its flicker burnishing gilt-edged picture frames and catching the rich brown lights of Eloise's hair as she moved about the room. She'd only been away for a few hours, but he missed her. Without her smile to light up his world, everything felt colder and Ross just stood there, his collar turned up and his back to Prospect House, as if the snowy expanse of white within had chilled him to the bone.

When Kym had redesigned his home, she'd talked a lot about inner peace and the beauty of nothing but Ross found himself reluctant to face the glare of the white walls of Prospect House. Neither did he fancy the look of the dark Downs where the dank trees dripped loneliness. He retreated back inside and poured a glass of red wine, then another, whilst the endless road of the evening stretched before him.

Finally, with nothing better to do, he switched on the TV. Another contemporary drama mining the seam of urban angst. Mindlessly, he watched as a beautiful woman in a tailored black coat, nipped in at her small waist to show off the lovely curve of her hips, tapped along a lonely street in glossy black high heels. A glorious camera composition of monotones was lifted by the flash of the red soles of her shoes as she picked up her pace, and the copper swish of her hair as she took frequent nervous glances over her shoulder, clearly suspicious that she was being followed.

'Behind you!' he drawled, swirling the crimson dregs in his glass. Was she completely ignorant of the conventions? Hadn't she read the rules of TV drama daring such an alluring young woman to walk night-time streets alone without punishment? The same old cliché, he decided, pouring himself another drink, and a particularly nasty one at that. He wiped his mouth, and, oh, there he was, her pursuer; hood raised, knife in pocket, his breath quickening as he narrowed the distance between himself and his prey. Really, was this what viewers wanted? A relentless tide of pretty girls being slaughtered on their screens?

Then the wine soured in his mouth, as Ross suddenly realised what he was watching. That's why it seemed so familiar. He'd ducked the issue until now, telling himself that his work belonged to everyone once it left his head and his hands, but this time he couldn't look away. This time he was face to face with an adaptation of one of his own novels. He flinched as the knife struck, then sat appalled by the depravity. What had happened to his subtle brush strokes and sparsely defined prose? Transformed by haunting music and lingering camera work, it had become something powerful, gripping and utterly profane. Was this what he had become? A man who traded on the mutilation and murder of women?

Ross tried to rationalise his horror, telling himself his authorial intention had been twisted. This sick, slick drama was no reflection of him as a man. The bottle of wine was mysteriously empty so Ross stumbled out to the kitchen to open a second, feeling the chill of the stainless steel worktops under cold white light. Back in the living room, the temperature seemed to have dropped too. A living room with no life. He poured another glass of wine

And then a worse thought occurred to him. In the beginning, writing had helped expunge the grief and hurt of the past, tamed his sometimes savage view of the world by sifting it through a creative sieve. Excavating that dark quarry had brought him success, money and career acclaim, yet left him unfulfilled. From the moment Eloise had stumbled into his arms, he had a sense of what was missing; she was now part of his present, but was she the key to his future? That very much depended on whether or not she had overcome her own demons, whether she could ever trust another man after being so desperately hurt by her husband.

Would it really have been so awkward for her to invite him to her family gathering today — or was it an excuse? He couldn't help but feel that she was withholding part of herself and he had a nasty feeling that the sick drama he'd just seen played out on his screen was the problem. Perhaps she was still suspicious of him, reluctant to have him around her happy normal family? Or maybe one of them had warned her off? Her dad had been quick to recognise him. Maybe her parents, after considering the matter, had concerns about their daughter hanging out with a man with the mind of a murderer?

A fugitive impression of lush feminine curves, tumbling hair and the scent of warm skin faded before he could define it and he wondered if Eloise was already lost to him. He closed his eyes and his glass fell from his hand, red wine spilling down his white sofa and across the expensive matting covering the floor.

★ ★ ★

Even Gracie seemed impatient to get up early this morning, propping her paws on the window sill and casting longing looks at Prospect House. For a dog who'd once been so phobic about men, she certainly had it bad. And no wonder, Ross was so kind, so considerate and so, so sexy . . . Eloise laughed. Yesterday, with her family, she'd felt very conscious of being on her own, for once, and decided that next time she'd definitely ask him along. That probably meant she had it bad too.

'Here's the thing, Gracie, I have to post a tapestry kit to a customer. It's still quite early so we could walk to the post office first and see Ross on our way back, or we could maybe call at Prospect House first and tell Ross to put the kettle on. What do you think?'

Gracie wagged her tail and gave an impatient little whine, turning her gaze from Eloise back to Prospect House.

'Good choice,' Eloise agreed, picking up her parcel. 'Why wait any longer? Come on, girl, let's go.'

Standing under the fretwork porch above Ross's front door, Eloise started to wonder if he had overslept or was unwell. This impression was confirmed when after what felt like an age, he opened the door, dishevelled, stubbled and wearing a shirt that had been buttoned hastily, affording her a tantalising glimpse of a hard, masculine chest dusted with dark hair.

'Eloise?' he said, as if she was someone he vaguely recognised. 'Do you want something?'

'Well, I *was* coming over to see if you fancied joining us for a walk,' she chortled, 'but it looks as if we've woken you up so it seems a bit harsh to drag you out into the cold. I wouldn't say no to a cup of tea though,' she added, with a winning smile. She waved her parcel at him, 'I'm just popping down to post this so why don't you put the kettle on while I pick up some croissants? I can tell you all about my brother-in-law's birthday over breakfast.'

Instead of looking pleased, Ross gave her a troubled stare and stroked Gracie's head in what was a rather perfunctory gesture.

'Eloise, do you mind if we don't.'

Her stomach plummeted as she realised how stupid she'd been to jump to conclusions. How very naïve of her to mistake old-fashioned lust for any-thing else. They'd slept together. That was it as far as he was concerned — wasn't that what he was trying to tell her? Of course he didn't want her rushing over there violating his privacy now that he'd scratched that particular itch. But the shock of his dismissal was brutal — he might have at least tried to be civil. She wasn't expecting breakfast in bed, but letting her down gently over a cup of tea would have been a lot kinder than sending her packing at the door. Bare branches sifted a bitter wind that stung her eyes as she glanced up towards the black windows of the tower.

'No, of course, I don't mind,' she said backing away slowly, before her feet refused to obey instructions. 'I expect you've got work to do.'

He threw her a grateful look, taking the lifeline she'd thrown him. 'Yes, that's it. I have, actually. We'll catch up some other time.'

'No problem,' she managed to grind out. 'I've got work to do too.'

As she turned and practically flew, tugging an unwilling Gracie with her in the direction of the post office, Eloise could feel his eyes on her back. She thought she heard him call her name but was too afraid that her tears would spill to turn round.

Arriving at the convenience store on legs that felt as if they belonged to someone else, Eloise was further dismayed to find Nigel from the garage in full flow to Mr and Mrs Khan who looked at her with grateful eyes hoping, no doubt, that Nigel would take the hint and leave.

'You'd think after pouring all that money into that bloody old house he'd want to stay, wouldn't you?' Nigel was telling them. 'I mean, he must have money to burn once you take into consideration estate agents' fees and solicitors. Not to mention the stamp duty on the next house. I don't think Hookfield's quite good enough for him. Says it's gone to the dogs. He's buying one of them executive houses the other side of the Downs towards Ebbesham. If he comes in though, don't say anything unless he does. He didn't put up a 'for sale' board or nothing — we'll have to wait until the 'sold' board goes up officially.'

Eloise felt what remaining colour she had left in her cheeks drain away. Ross was moving — even worse, Ross had quietly put his house up for sale without even mentioning it to her. Of course he didn't have to worry about being polite to her any more — he was practically off the scene!

'Looking a bit peaky, girl,' Nigel said on the way past. 'About time you ditched the dog and got yourself a fella instead.'

★   ★   ★

Having cried herself out, Eloise decided at last that there was no reason for both of them to feel miserable so she poured a rare treat of milky tea into a bowl for Gracie and allowed her a sweet biscuit. When she lit the fire too, Gracie was completely content; she pirouetted with pleasure before tucking her tail in and settling herself down. Eloise watched distractedly as her body relaxed and she fell asleep. If only she could be more like the relaxed creature at her feet; all Eloise knew about the untold horrors Gracie had suffered in her past was that she'd been tied to a post with an injured shoulder that someone, presumably, was disinclined to pay for, then left to die in the snow.

The people who found her had taken her to a vet who'd suggested the kindest thing might be to put her out of her misery but, thankfully, a greyhound rescue centre had been able to take her in. Eloise wiped away the tear that slid down her cheek, and blew out a long breath, thinking how close the animal had come to death, how much poorer her life would be without Gracie in it. The first few months together had been difficult, painful too, but they had learned to trust and love each other. Another tear trickled down her face. If only she could learn from Gracie's example; forget the past and move on.

Gracie's love had enriched her life, but it wasn't enough to stop her experiencing loneliness of a different kind, nor from yearning for human love and affection. But once again, she had managed to pick the wrong type of man, someone who wasn't in it for the long haul. She was in deep enough, but at least she found out what a short attention span Ross had before she'd made a complete fool of herself. Really she should be grateful he hadn't pressed the point about meeting her entire family or she'd be the object of their pity and concern all over again. And it was a good thing he was moving instead of hanging around like a bad smell, a constant reminder of her disastrous one-night-stand. How typical of her luck, though, that just as she had hopes of building a new life, the person she thought she could build it with had dashed it to pieces.

Drained and exhausted, Eloise closed her eyes and felt her body succumb to the warmth of the room as she drifted off to sleep. When, eventually, her eyes flicked open she found Gracie watching her with a long, unblinking look of devotion which suddenly made the lack of human contact seem a little less important. 'Silly sausage,' she muttered fondly. Gracie quivered with pleasure and they both settled down for another snooze, sighing in unison.

It was a massive effort the next morning to leave the house but Gracie was keen and, just because Eloise felt like hiding, didn't mean Gracie had to suffer too. Spring had retreated into itself again, giving way to heavy rain in the night which had turned the usual tracks to mud. Nevertheless, she still had to earn a living and focus on her new collection of designs, although it was hard to think of anything to inspire her work in the current climate when she was hoping for ideas that were brighter, more optimistic.

Despite telling herself that what Ross did next was no business of hers, she nevertheless found herself gravitating towards one of Ebbesham's leafier and most prestigious wards on the other side of the Downs. Her parents had always lived in Ebbesham so her memories, from the earliest age, were steeped in the area, but even in that short span of time, changes were taking place almost daily. Before the roads widened and dropped down to the town, a horseshoe of new 'executive' properties had sprung up which, despite the builders' painfully contrived efforts at individuality, all looked exactly the same. Why on earth would Ross prefer one of these to the eccentric charms of Prospect House?

Standing in front of them, Eloise silently grieved for the racing stables which occupied the land when she was a little girl. Instead of 'The Hurlingham', a four bedroom detached home with en-suite facilities and choice of designer tiles, she imagined a field and remembered watching a new intake of autumn yearlings, riderless, but each one bearing the weight of so many hopes and dreams.

As a teenager, she still liked to return to watch those thoroughbred babies being taken through their first expensive paces whenever she could. Imagine, she often thought, the sheer exhilaration of shaping a potential winner. And as much as she tried to tell herself that the new homes represented an equally auspicious future with families and new babies and different promises waiting to be fulfilled, she still couldn't see what attractions this anonymous estate held for someone who needed his own company as much as Ross.

Gracie shivered at her side and Eloise dredged herself away from the silt of the past, the snorting horses and the aroma of dung, to gaze once more upon the sterile Hurlingham. 'Come on girl, let's go home.' She smiled and as she bent to stroke Gracie's head, the animal licked her wrist to welcome her back.

Ducking back into the woods, where fallen copper leaves shimmered against the loamy soil and grey-green lichens garnished bare branches, Eloise still didn't feel inspired enough even to come up with a few sketches. Perhaps she could follow Ross's example and try something more macabre?

Maybe, she thought, she would attract a new breed of embroiderers; punters who might be charmed by a composition inspired by the dead twig in front of her with its gruesome fleshy fungus like a disembodied human ear. Bending closer she had to reassure herself that it wasn't an ear and even when she was quite sure that it had never belonged to anyone, her mind refused to clear the image.

She'd heard that back in the Seventies the body of a prostitute was found round here. Not a local girl but someone who'd pushed her luck too far one night, ignored her warning instincts and got into a car with the wrong man. A man unknown to this day. Someone who knew that he could take his time in a place where courting couples in their steamed-up cars were ignored. Someone, for all she knew, still living in the area.

Eloise picked up her pace. This was the loneliest part of the track. Shortly it would rejoin the main path but, at this point, she knew that she could not be seen and her mouth was so dry that she didn't think she could scream if she wanted to. Not that she did want to. Birds hopped nervously to other perches as she passed and every twig that snapped seemed to be coming from behind her.

By the time the track widened out again, Eloise had got herself in such a state she was ready to kiss the ground. What on earth had made her feel so nervous? Getting edgy about the solitary walks, which were such a rich source of material for her work, was something she just couldn't afford to do. Nevertheless, she was greatly relieved to see the open space ahead. Taking a final glance over her shoulder, she was just congratulating herself for resisting the impulse to dart towards it, when she noticed the outline of a figure moving stealthily through the very last group of trees.

A bolt of sheer terror went through her and she shamelessly ran out towards the clearing. Gracie, thinking it was a great game, bounced beside her looking so delighted that Eloise wondered if it was only her imagination working overtime after all. Turning boldly, she scrutinised the wooded copse for any sign of activity, laughing at herself when there was none. And then she turned and felt heat, movement and the smell of sweat and adrenaline-pumped fear as a burly form lunged towards her.

11

It was lunchtime when Ross sat back in his chair and stretched his aching back after his writing marathon. Finally — when he'd almost got beyond hope of ever producing another novel — he had a synopsis, an outline plan and a couple of draft chapters. The idea had suggested itself to him in restless sleep, becoming so insistent that he'd stumbled into his study and let it pour forth. Satisfied that, at last, he'd captured the essence of the story without losing the freshness of that sudden flash of inspiration, he could afford to let it run in the background of his mind whilst he caught up with real life.

But first, he thought, pushing back his hair, it was time for a much-needed shower before celebrating with his two favourite girls. When Eloise had called at his door only the day before, he had been so deep in his imaginary world that he'd been completely disoriented and distracted. He had a feeling he might even have been a bit offhand. With hindsight, he should perhaps have explained that he was writing again, but he was sure she'd be pleased for him once she understood why he'd been so eager to get back to his desk.

* ★ *

Raring to go after his ablutions, Ross grabbed a bottle of champagne out of the fridge and was just looking across the road to see if there was any sign of Eloise when he noticed a van pulling up outside and his new Best Fan, Amy Merry, the animal warden, clambered out. Ross ducked away from the window, praying she hadn't seen him. Just when he'd decided the coast was clear, there was a thunderous knock at the door. How rude. Well, he'd just have to tell Ms Merry he was working — even if part of him was half-tempted to run his latest idea past her for some instant feedback. He had a feeling that the new book might not be as popular with his old fans as its predecessors.

Dismissing the idea quickly, he opened the door with a suitably unwelcoming glare, and was chastened to see Eloise wilt as she took the full force of his unfriendliness. She took a step back.

'Oh sweetheart,' he said hastily, 'that wasn't meant for you. I had something far more pleasant in mind to share with you. I was just going to see if I could tempt you with a bottle of champagne.'

'To celebrate your next move, I guess,' she muttered, her bottom lip trembling before she blurted out, 'I'm really sorry to bother you Ross, but it'll take too long for my parents to get here and I don't know who else to turn to. I really need your help; Gracie's missing.'

At once, he noticed a tear sliding down her cheek. Her long coat was caked with mud, and blood was trickling from a graze on the palm of her hand. 'I'll go,' he told her, 'but you should stay here and wash that cut.'

'There's no time,' she said, producing a none-too-clean tissue from a pocket and dabbing her hand with it. 'I think Brett Dorling-Jones's reported me to the animal warden. Her van's here so we've got to find Gracie before she does. If Gracie's found wandering round loose, she could be picked up as a stray and taken into council kennels. But I'm even more afraid of what could happen if she panics and attacks someone, she could be . . . '

Ross grabbed her and hugged her to his chest, his heart aching for her as she stifled a sob. 'It won't come to that, I promise.' He certainly hoped not. And if any harm came to Gracie because of his dog-hating neighbour, he might not be responsible for his actions. 'We'll find her. Two seconds,' he said, sliding his feet into his boots by the front door and grabbing a coat from the stand. 'But why would Brett know Gracie was loose? What happened?'

'It was all my fault.' Eloise said, skidding as they reached the slippery track. Ross grabbed her arm and held on to her. 'We'd walked further than usual and I was tired and not thinking straight and I got myself in a panic because I thought someone was lurking in the trees. I freaked and ran towards the clearing and I didn't see Brett until it was too late.'

'You mean he attacked you?' Ross blazed with anger.

'No. Nothing like that. We went headlong into each other. I fell flat on my front and Brett somersaulted over me. He's not best pleased I can tell you — his new high visibility jacket got torn and he says he's going to send me the bill for a replacement.'

'And Gracie?'

He heard Eloise struggle to swallow the lump in her throat. 'I dropped the lead when I fell over and she was so upset when Brett started shouting, she took off. Ross, she was really sprinting — she could be anywhere by now. What if she breaks a leg or reaches the main road and gets run over? I'd never forgive myself. I've been calling for her but either she can't hear me or she's too afraid to respond.'

The hum of the main road carrying towards them on the breeze sounded particularly ominous, but what if Gracie hadn't got that far? 'What did Brett do when Gracie ran off?'

'I wasn't looking,' Eloise replied, scanning the vast swathe of the Downs stretching out in front of them. She turned back and looked up at him with troubled eyes. 'He's a bit rough and ready and he certainly doesn't like dogs, but he works hard for his family. I've just got to trust that he wouldn't do anything that would create trouble for them.'

He hoped her trust wasn't misplaced. 'Wherever Gracie is, we'll find her,' Ross assured her.

After an hour of fruitless searching, Ross was getting frustrated. Closed doors opened for him. Elusive executives, exclusive venues and hip restaurants always found a place for him, but the Downs with its secretive copses and unstoppable tide of brambles refused to give up one skinny dog.

'I hope she hasn't been stolen,' Eloise worried as they started to retrace their footsteps.

'Not likely, is it?' he tried to reassure her. 'I thought there were dozens of unwanted greyhounds — why would anyone want to steal Gracie?'

'It's an anomaly, but strangely they're one of the breeds most at risk from dognappers. They're sometimes stolen for use in illegal hare coursing, or maybe for breeding. In either case, you can imagine what happens to them if they don't perform.'

Ross didn't want to think about it. He called Gracie's name yet again, but there was no response. Footsore and weary and with no sign of the greyhound anywhere, he suggested that they made their way back to Prospect House to try a different tactic. 'We'll try phoning vets to see if she's been brought in,' he suggested. 'It doesn't mean we've given up, but you need to take a break before you drop.'

Eloise looked momentarily crestfallen before brightening up at the thought that Gracie might have beaten them back and could be there waiting for them. Privately, Ross feared the worst. The likeliest scenario was that Gracie had got out onto the main road where anything could have happened to her. But as they reached the muddy track which led back down to Hookfield, they could both see Amy Merry's van and two figures waiting beside it.

'You bastard,' said Ross, springing at Brett.

'Oi!' said Brett. 'I'm trying to help, here. You should be thanking me for sorting that dog out.'

Ross's fists tightened on Brett's collar. 'What have you done?'

'Let go of that man,' said the animal warden, 'or I'll call the police and have you arrested for assault. I can see where you get your sick ideas from now.'

Charming, thought Ross, who's the villain here?

'Gracie!' Eloise shrieked. 'She's in the van. Oh god, you're not going to have her destroyed are you?'

'I'm trying to keep her safe!' the animal warden retorted. 'This gentleman called me to say that there had been a minor incident, but that if I found a stray greyhound on my rounds that it had a loving home here and had escaped through no fault of its own. Whilst you two have been enjoying your leisurely stroll, this poor animal came home looking for comfort and fortunately I was able to get her into the back of the van and settle her down.'

'But I thought you hated dogs!' Eloise said to Brett.

'I bloody do, but I'm not entirely made of stone. Got three kiddies of my own, 'aven't I, who are desperate for a pet. Mind you, I think they'll be getting something smaller, like a hamster, when we move.'

'You're moving too?' Eloise asked slowly.

'Well I don't know who else is moving, but I've had enough of it round here. Me and the missus have got one of them posh new houses on that new Ebbesham estate. It's not so far for the missus to take the girls to their private school either. As for your bloody dog — call it my good deed before I move. I know we've had our differences but I didn't want it to end on a sour note. Anyway, I've stood round here freezing my nuts off long enough, the family'll be wondering where I am.'

Ross was glad he hadn't punched his neighbour's lights out although, despite Brett's apparent change of character, he still didn't trust him further than he could throw him and would be glad to see the back of him. He also hoped that Amy Merry hadn't noticed Gracie trying to snap at Brett's heels when she was released from the van.

Then it was just the three of them. He wrapped his arm round Eloise's shoulders, took Gracie's lead with his other arm and marched them over to

Prospect House.

'Just wait a minute.' Eloise drew back from him as they were about to cross the threshold. 'You've tramped all over the Downs with me to get Gracie back. You don't need to do anything else. Thank you, but Gracie and I will be fine now.'

Ross scratched his head. 'I know you *will* be fine, but you're both looking pretty shaken at the moment. Eloise, please, you don't always have to be on your guard. I thought we'd shared enough by now for you to trust me. Don't you know how much you both mean to me? Please don't pull up the drawbridge now.'

He heard her take a deep breath. Gracie tucked herself in next to her mistress and they both regarded him with serious dark eyes.

'Before I go any further,' Eloise said at last, 'I need to know what I did wrong. Why were you so odd with me yesterday morning?'

'*You've* done nothing wrong,' he said,

struggling to speak through a throat that was suddenly tight with emotion when he remembered how much she'd been hurt in the past. 'I'm the selfish idiot, the one who didn't take enough time to tell you what was going on. Please will you come in, Eloise? Because you and Gracie look ready to drop and we've got a lot of ground to cover.'

'Of course,' she replied, still looking miserable as they walked into the hall. 'You're moving aren't you? I heard Nigel tell Mr and Mrs Khan about it. But, gosh, how ironic that you'll still have Brett as a neighbour.'

'Eloise,' Ross said patiently. 'You misunderstood. It's Brett and his family who are the ones who are moving. Not me. I meant to tell you the good news after I called in at the petrol station on Sunday when you were at your parents. Nigel told me. They're looking for a better class of neighbour, apparently, not some layabout like me 'sitting around on his arse all day with no visible means of support.''

Eloise giggled, 'Oh well they got that bit right. But why didn't you tell me sooner?'

'So many questions,' Ross said, kissing her neck and helping her out of her first layer of clothes. 'And you'll get all the answers. But first I'm running you a long bath where you're to relax whilst I sort Gracie out. You'd better give me your keys and a list of things you're going to need for the night. We'll have plenty of time because I'm not going anywhere. In fact, if anyone else is moving, it'll be you and Gracie. You can move in here where I can keep an eye on you both — this house is far too bloody cold and lonely for one.'

* * *

A little over seven months later, Eloise watched the autumn sunshine streaming through the stained glass, sending little squares of red, gold and blue over Ross's sleeping form. Gone was every trace of chilly white. Now the walls of the turret bedroom were the rosy pink of dawn and gilded with sunlight shimmering through the doors that opened to the narrow cast-iron balcony girdling the tower. Lying still, she could hear the whisper of young leaves unfurling in the breeze and observe the golden wash of first light, slowly giving way to a promising blue sky. It was a lovely room; romantic and wild. A place to sleep, to dream and — she grinned when she realised Ross had come to and was watching her with dark, mischievous eyes — the perfect place for making love.

'You know we really should get up before your family turn up and find us still in bed,' he said, much, much later.

'Oh, I don't think that would surprise them.' Eloise laughed, being careful to avoid stepping on Gracie as she slipped out of bed.

'All the same, I'd rather not get in your parents' bad books, having finally completed a not-so-bad book of my own.'

'It's brilliant! Well worth all the angst

it caused when I called at your door and got the brush-off.'

'Hey!' he protested, 'I was in the zone — just the way you are when you're creating a new design.'

Eloise flicked her hair back from her shoulders, thinking what a relief it was to live with someone who understood the importance of capturing an elusive idea with speed and stealth. Seb had always resented it and complained that her designs were more important to her than him.

'Do you think your mum will approve of the new novel?'

'Ross, you know your approval rating couldn't rise any higher! They love telling their friends that a best-selling author is practically one of the family!' She perched on the edge of his side of the bed and wrapped her arms round his deliciously naked muscular shoulders. 'I'm just relieved that your publishers like it so much. You took a big risk changing direction. Not to mention killing off your hero like that. The 'Finn' fans will be protesting all over the internet,' she added, wondering how the loss of such a popular fictional detective would be received.

'How do you know he's dead?' Ross asked, slyly.

'I can't imagine how he'd survive his boat capsizing in the middle of the Atlantic like that,' Eloise pointed out.

'Ah, but his body hasn't been found, has it? Anyway, I'd had enough of Finn and his appetite for bloodthirsty murders, it's his girlfriend's turn now. Cass will be following some very mysterious leads when she tries to discover what happened.'

'From dark thrillers to spine-chillers. Perhaps you'll try your hand at romance one day?'

'I'm doing my best.' He smiled. 'And talking of happy ever afters, I wanted to show you this before your family arrive.'

'Ooh, Ross,' she squealed, 'I don't think we've got time have we?'

'Be serious, will you? I just hope Gracie hasn't eaten it.'

He fumbled worriedly under the bed until he found what he was searching for. 'Now close your eyes and hold out your hand.'

Gracie, sensing she was being left out, shuffled round to rest her soft chin on Eloise's thigh, reminding them she was still there.

'Don't peep,' Ross chided her, taking her hand and sliding a ring on to her left finger. 'There. Now you can look.'

Eloise gasped as the sunlight caught the solitaire glittering like a star on her hand.

'What do you think?' Ross asked shyly.

'Oh Ross,' she breathed, lifting her gaze from the diamond, shimmering like a rainbow through her tears. 'I don't know how to thank you.'

'You don't need to thank me, silly. You just have to say — '

'Yes!' she said, throwing her arms round his neck and pulling him towards her. Until Ross had come along, she had firmly decided that the only faithful companion she would ever have in her life was Gracie. Love, she thought, was only true in fairy tales. But Ross had changed her mind. Now she was a believer.

BLUEPRINT FOR LOVE

Henriette Gyland

Hazel Dobson is pleased when she gets temp work at Gough Associates, an architectural company based in a beautiful manor house in Norfolk. While it's a far cry from the bright lights of London, she is keen to get away from a mundane job with a lecherous boss, and to spend some time with her great-aunt. There she meets handsome and wealthy Jonathan Gough, and sees a chance at happiness and a family with him. But some people just don't want Hazel and Jonathan to be happy . . .

LAKELAND INTERLUDE

Jean M. Long

Following a painful break-up, Casey Brett decides to start a new life in the Lake District as an assistant in her friend Flora's Dance and Drama Studio. But it's not all plain sailing, as a fellow instructor feels Casey is stepping on her toes, she receives the unwanted romantic attentions of a local hiking guide, and she loses several of her most promising students. But she also meets wealthy businessman Blake Lawley, and feels an instant frisson. Can Casey overcome her problems and find happiness in her new home?

THE TIME OF THE FLOOD

Miranda Barnes

The Northumbrian village of Carlton is hit by unprecedented flooding when torrential rain overwhelms its defences and the river bursts its banks. During a long and difficult night, Anna Mason and her friend David Wilson work together to help the needy. Meanwhile, moody Gregory McKenzie, the attractive visiting grandson of one of the villagers, shows a previously unsuspected side to his character. But the flood will also wash away decades of secrecy, unearthing old family mysteries . . .

THE GHOST OF GLENDALE

Natalie Kleinman

Phoebe Marcham is resigned to spinsterhood, unwilling to settle for less than the deep love her parents shared. Then adventurer Duncan Armstrong rides into her home wood, with laughter in his eyes and more charm in his little finger than anyone she has ever met before. Far from ridiculing her family ghost, Duncan resolves to help solve the mystery that has left Simon Marcham a soul in torment for two hundred years. Will they be able to put the ghost to rest — and find love together?

THE WEDDING REJECT TABLE

Angela Britnell

When Maggie Taylor, a cake decorator, and Chad Robertson, a lawyer from Nashville, meet at a wedding in Cornwall, it's not under the best circumstances. They have both been assigned to 'the reject table' alongside a toxic collection of grumpy great-aunts, bitter divorcées and stuffy organists. Maggie has grown used to being the reject, though when Chad helps her out of a wedding cake disaster she begins to wonder whether the future could hold more for her. But will Chad be strong enough to deal with the other problems in Maggie's life?